HERE ON OLD ROUTE 7

HERE ON OLD ROUTE 7

STORIES BY

JOAN CONNOR

University of Missouri Press

COLUMBIA AND LONDON

Library of Congress Cataloging-in-Publication Data

Connor, Joan.
    Here on Old Route 7 : stories / by Joan Connor.
        p.   cm.
    Contents: Old Route 7 — Camp — The attic — Good neighbors —
Aaron's rod — The ten joyful mysteries of the one true faith — A hard
place — Devil's fiddle — When mountains move.
    ISBN 0-8262-1129-1 (paper : alk. paper)
    I. Title
PS3553.0514255H47   1997
813'.54—dc21   97-15900
                                                                    CIP

∞ ™ This paper meets the requirements of the
American National Standard for Permanence of Paper
for Printed Library Materials, Z39.48, 1984.

Designer: Mindy Shouse
Typesetter: BOOKCOMP
Printer and binder: Thomson-Shore, Inc.
Typefaces: Copperplate33bc, Minion

For acknowledgments, see page 137.

For my family in order of their appearance:

Walker, Mary, Peter,
Daniel and Marlene Connor,
Michele Reid, Kerry Wessell,
and David Holton.

On the other hand, to hell with the sequoias.

CONTENTS

Here on Old Route 7

OLD ROUTE 7

A ROAD RUNS BECAUSE IT HAS TO

OLD ROUTE 7 RUNS PARALLEL to Cold River Road. The river runs between. Along the road derelict elm trees rot between salt-eaten maples. The road crews don't come out here anymore to cut the branches back. The maples arch over the road, their trunks nicked by plows or gashed by lightning, lichened and molding. The road runs from nowhere to nowhere. It runs like the road in the old story; "you can't get there from here." It runs like an old river, by natural process, circling back on itself, cutting itself off until it stops running altogether, as separate and still as an oxbow.

If a road had a will, if a road had any sense at all, it would run away from here. But a road has no sense. A road runs where a road runs. Like a passive passenger, it arrives at its isolation through a deterministic process—as if it were its own destination.

The cars that drive over old Route 7, over its blistered tar and potholes, its frost heaves and irrational curves, are rusted-out, Bondo-patched Falcons, old Chevys with tin can mufflers and bald tires. They know the road. Their odometers spin round back to zero. Their rearview mirrors reflect what's going by, what's gone. Their retreads circle round and round like the hands of a clock winding down. They know the road.

The road runs smack into a dead end where it hooks into the sleek four-lane highway with entrance ramps, merges, acceleration and passing lanes, the new Route 7. Cars with ski racks and bicycle racks and luggage racks whir down the new road, passing the old one by.

1

Beyond the hook, old Route 7 doesn't run. Beyond the black and yellow stripes of the road blockade, the old tar crumples. Plants root there, poke through the pavement as if tar were loam.

Old Route 7 runs only twenty miles. People live there.

Anna Bonay pulls her cardigan closer around her shoulders. The late afternoon sun does not warm her. The sky deepens beyond blue into the pale purple of asters, the color of her eyes. At her age, the sharp edge of fall always cuts into the air. But she likes the fall. She likes the purple clouds of asters. They hide the rotting corner post of number four, the broken tricycles and dismembered baby dolls in the dirt yard down by six. She likes the scent of leaves burning, likes their litter on the ground, carpeting the holes in the tarmac of the parking lot, covering the cracks in the sidewalk, the loose mortar of the brick foundation of the office building. The place looks like a dump, and she depends on nature to disguise it. When the asters and leaves fail, the snow falls. When the snow melts, the lilacs thicken and bloom. When the lilacs go by. . . . But Anna hesitates for the lilacs, heart-shaped leaves, clusters of blossoms, bunchy as grapes. The lilacs startle into bloom, and Paulie's there. . . .

———

He tugged on her hand. "I want to show you something," he said. And she laughed, smelling the purple perfume of the lilacs lingering in her hair, and she followed him toward the river. The ground, still wet, sucked at their shoes. When they reached the river bank, Paulie turned and waved his arm toward Route 7. "What do you see?" he asked.

And she looked at Paulie, his hair coiled tight and light as fleece, his eyes and brows so dark. "Are you having me on, Paulie?" she asked.

"No, no," he said. "Tell me what you see."

"I see an old barn," Anna said.

"We bulldoze the barn to ground. Then what do you see?" he asked.

"I see the road?" she asked uncertainly.

"Right," he said, "the road. And the road brings cars, and the cars bring people, and the people are tired. And where do they sleep?"

"In their cars?" Anna guessed.

"No they don't," Paulie said, and he threw his arms around her waist. "They sleep, Anna, in the Sunset Motor Cabins Court."

"You're crazy," she said, but she laughed as if his craziness made her happy.

Paulie took all the money he saved before the war and the money his father fronted him, and he went to the First National Bank, and he

3

got the mortgage and he bought the land. First off, he raised the sign. The pole towered over the road, arching toward the top. He cut the sign himself, circular, with a jigsaw, and hand lettered it with black paint. He hoisted it up with ropes and pulleys on the white pole. "A sign's very important," he said. "It makes a statement. No neon—we're a family place. That's what that sign says. 'Your home away from home.'" He was proud of that sign.

Then they razed the barn and raised the office building. Paulie's father helped with the foundation work. That first winter, they did the interior work on their apartment, tucked behind the main desk, and, in the spring, constructed the cabins one by one, one through six. Paulie contracted little of the work, just the electrical and some of the plumbing. He learned on the job as he went along, framing, clapboarding, laying the floors. When the cabins were completed, he teased Anna, "We'll have as many kids, and then we'll build another half-dozen. America's on the move," he said, "and we're moving with it." In the early years of their marriage, it was one of his favorite expressions.

Anna prospered behind the desk. She washed the speckled linoleum in the kitchen with Spic and Span. She wiped down the new electric icebox with vinegar and water. She scoured the cast iron rings of the gas stove. She baked tuna noodle hot dish and hamburger casserole. She plumped the cushions on the hide-a-bed divan. Everything sparkled, new and clean as morning sun.

When the guests arrived, she registered their names in neat ledgers. She issued keys and made change for the pop machine. She made up the beds of the cabins with hospital corners, emptied the wastebaskets, swept the porch floors. She watched the guests come, sticky and tired, children whining. She watched them go in a rustle of roadmaps and luggage checks, anxious to be on the road. Go and come. Come and go. She and Paulie wanted children, but their children did not come.

"Never mind," Paulie said. "We're a happy enough family, just us two. And we're on the move."

Anna picks lavender lint from her sweater. She slumps slightly lower in her chair adjusting to the narrowing angle of afternoon light. Siege, over in number four, complained about dirty towels this morning. Her legs ache. She sags at the prospect of lugging the laundry over to the

Coin-a-matic at the Grand Union Plaza. Siege just has to wait. This isn't a hotel.

Maybe, she thinks, it wasn't exactly like her memory, but it was almost like that—her, a happy young wife busily burning Sunbeam bread in the Sunbeam toaster. Paulie, an eager young man, always on the move, his toolbox in hand, adjusting screen door springs, replacing fuses, raking the courtyard. But, even then, there were problems. The flat roof of the office leaked under the weight of snow. The cabin plumbing froze and split the pipes.

"Anna," he said, "hand me the monkey wrench."

She handed him the vise grip.

"The monkey wrench." Water spurted in Paulie's face.

She hesitated. Monkey wrench. Hammer. Screwdriver.

"Dumb dump-picker. Don't stand there catching flies. Give me the wrench."

Paulie wasn't usually unkind. Even when they were kids, and Red Switchel would toss stones at her and chant, "Anna banana peel. Flies on her skin. Smells like the dump that her dad works in," Paulie didn't join in.

Paulie was her cousin, a Bonay too, but not a dump Bonay. Paulie's daddy was a mason. Even as a kid, Paulie thought a man could build himself up, better himself. Paulie walked tall when he carried her books for her. "Don't listen to that trash," he said. "They'll never amount to nothing."

The kids called Anna "Boney," but her name was pronounced *Bonay*. It was French.

Poppa Bonay worked as the dump man, the attendant at the dump. They lived in a house, a shack really, built almost entirely of junked doors, a few odd windows, and corrugated tin salvaged from the dump. Their yard sprouted a viny tangle of bedsprings, stumps of stacked wheel rims, a scrub growth of broken axles, boxes of deposit bottles, and tattered *Look* magazines instead of trees and grass.

Poppa got first pickings at the dump, uncovering fur cuffs and felt hats and off-sized shoes for his Anna.

"Poppa, I can't wear this. The children laugh at me."

"So what is wrong with it?" He pinched the silky, nylon dress in his fingers.

"It's too big. It's for an old lady. It isn't mine."

"All of this is ours," Poppa Bonay said and grinned, gaptoothed. "We are rich in hidden assets." And he gestured grandly toward the dump.

"They make fun of me. They call me 'ragpicker Boney.'"

"A dump is nothing to be ashamed of," Poppa said. "Who makes the trash? We don't. They do. You can read somebody from their trash. See," he said, and he lifted up a bottle, "Mrs. Tanner dyes her hair. The Tarbell dog has worms." He studied a scrap of paper. "The Crawfords have money in the bank. A dump is a history book, see?" he said.

Anna stared at him, at his glittery black eyes, his stocking cap, the red and black checkerboard of his wool jacket.

"Might be a good catch for you, that Crawford boy," he said.

"Oh Poppa, you do not understand." She ran into the shack, crying. And he called after her, "I am not only the dump man. I am an archivist."

On Fridays Bonay took his paycheck to the general store in town and bought cans of Del Monte vegetables, a string of frankfurters, a box of bridge mix chocolates, and a six of Black Label. On Friday night he drank himself quietly into a stupor. Saturdays were busy at the dump.

Poppa could say what he liked, but Anna knew. A dump-picker was a dump-picker, and you couldn't change that just like you couldn't change the name of Dump Road. The town could put up all the signs they wanted to saying "Deer Leap Road." They could hang a sign calling it Madison Avenue if they wanted, but people would still call it Dump Road. You couldn't change people or how they thought.

Although Paulie sure tried. Paulie returned from the war, a sergeant, dedicated to a purposeful fulfillment of the life he'd escaped with, and certain of two things: that a hardworking man could pull himself up, move through the ranks, and that America was on the move.

But Anna was not; she was still. She stood next to the old scale on the porch of the general store with a box of Wheaties in her hand. Paulie did not see her at first. He cranked the pump handle. He removed his uniform jacket and hitched his trousers up slightly at the knees before crouching to put gas into the black Dodge. Only then did he look up.

"Hi Paulie," Anna said, then fell silent before this near stranger, who stood up so tall and crisp.

"Well, Anna Bonay," Paulie said. "Don't you look fine, pretty as a magazine cover." And he approached her, his hand extended. When she did not take his hand, he reached past her, picked up one of the scale weights and tested its heft in the palm of his hand. "Anna Bonay," he said again and slipped the weight back on the bar. He finished pumping the gas and slid his arms back into his jacket. He strolled over to the big, red Coke cooler on the porch and dropped a nickel in the slot. "Can I get you a Coke, Anna?" he asked as he fished a bottle out of the water for himself.

Anna shook her head. Paulie plucked at the knees of his trousers and sat down on the slatted bench and smiled up at her. "Nice day for a drive, don't you think?" he asked. And Anna nodded.

When Anna told Poppa Bonay she was going to marry Paulie, he said, "Your children will all be fools, but that hasn't stopped a Bonay yet. You pregnant?" he asked.

And she shook her head.

"One man's treasure is another man's trash," Poppa said, by way of marital blessing.

And Anna and Paulie were married. They moved in behind the desk of the Sunset Court office, and for a while Anna believed with Paulie, things were looking up.

Paulie had a knack of raising Anna up to his beliefs, of hoisting her spirits as easily as he'd raised the Sunset sign. But he could lower her, too, worry her . . .

———

Anna buttons her cardigan. She hears the scuffle of feet through the leaves across what had been the site of cabin five. Maria is back with the kids. Anna hears the jabber she cannot understand. The light, low in the sky, lengthens the shadow cast by the splintered stump of the signpost. The shadow marks time like a sundial on the concrete pad Paulie poured. Paulie would have hated to see it fractured like this. He always was the neat one of the marriage. Anna had tried to keep things up at first when everything was new, but things just got dirty again, and after a while she no longer bothered. But Paulie sure would hate to see everything so dingy, so rundown, the cabins needing paint, the tarmac cracked, the signpost still split from that day. Anna shudders. She wants to go inside, but her legs do not move. They seem to have a will of their own these days. They don't cooperate, as if they've lost their spirit.

When things got tough, Paulie kept his spirits up. At night he'd take her out to Dave's Twilight Drive-In. Nestled in the front seat of the Dodge, a blanket tossed over the cracked vinyl of the seat, he'd say, "We're going to weather this thing. We can beat it." But he worried. Anna knew. Once he drove off with the speaker box still clamped to the window. He offered Dave money for the damage, but Dave waved Paulie off. Dave was like that.

Sometimes she and Paulie went drinking at Siege's Quonset hut. Siege operated the dance hall then. He called it the Moondust Ballroom. All the chairs and linen-covered tables hugged the curving walls. Short candles burned under glass on all the tables. Siege booked local orchestras—Carl Kurlanski and the Big Time Band every Friday night. Paulie didn't dance, but Red Switchel did—with everyone but his wife. He taught Anna the fox-trot, his hands slipping down until she had to slap them back out of harm's way. While she danced, she hunted for Paulie's eyes, lost to her in a galaxy of strangers, in the flecks of light twirling from the mirrored globe on the ceiling, as vain as searching for a single star in the Milky Way.

They drank seven and sevens. Sometimes Siege would stand them to a drink and join them at their table. He and Paulie would talk business.

"You're packing them in tonight," Paulie said.

"Yeah," Siege said, "but if they reroute Route 7 like they're talking about, we'll take it in the shorts."

"They'll never get it through," Paulie said. "And even if they do, it'll be years before they start construction around here. We'll all have time to land on our feet." But Paulie's dark brows furrowed.

Siege slid the paper wrapping down his straw into a cylinder of accordion pleats. "You a snake charmer, Anna?" he asked. He dropped a drop of seven and seven on the wrinkled round of paper, and it curled away from itself, arching, crawling, opening up. "Yup, she's a charmer all right. But watch out for old Red, eh Paulie? He's a snake if one ever shed a skin."

"That's what his wife says," Paulie said and chuckled. Siege was okay in Paulie's book.

Anna lowered her eyes. The wrapper, puddled in the seven and seven, dissolved with dampness like a dirty tissue.

Contrary to Paulie's predictions, the road crews began construction.

Once a week Paulie attended the hearings with Siege and Dave. Paulie brought progress reports home to Anna. "They're going to bypass our stretch of road," he said. "But, by God, we're not beat yet. This is America. People have a say. It's the squeaky wheel that gets the oil."

And at night when he came home from his meetings, Anna looked at his face to read the news there. The news was bad, but she could see Paulie was not broken yet. His eyes still looked up. His eyes still had fight in them. And she asked him no questions, even when the mortgage bills began accumulating in the cubby below the registration desk, carefully slit open, dated, and filed.

"We're going to weather this thing," Paulie said.

Paulie managed to get a sign situated at the intersection with new Route 7 approved by the town council. It was smaller than the one he'd built, but it spelled out clearly for passing traffic, "Sunset Motor Cabins Court," with an arrow indicating the direction and the route, Alternate Route 7.

"People will still come," Paulie said. "Some families like the quiet. We've got the view of the river. They can't reroute the river." And some people did come, but not enough. "Maybe we should change the name of the place," Paulie said, "capitalize on the river, like, 'River View Motor Court—Cabins.' " But Paulie did not paint a new sign.

And one day, his face almost gray, he said, "Anna, things are bad. I think we can get through this slump if we auction off a couple of the cabins."

Pioneer Playground and Petting Zoo, a kids' camp, bought two of the cabins, five and three (Paulie didn't want to upset the original layout too much). Huge flatbed tractor-trailers hauled the cabins away. It was a big operation. But the money barely saw them through the winter.

Then Paulie came up with the idea of long-term rentals. "Money we could count on every month," he said. That was how Siege came to live in four.

Neighbors were kind. Red stopped by and joked around. Dave came by, but he didn't know what to say, just stood there like Dave does, hulking like he's too big for his own body, his porkpie hat crunched in his fist.

Anna thanked them for their kindness, and she studied Paulie's face. Would he break? Because if Paulie didn't break, they would be okay. She brought him his coffee, regular, in the morning, and she handed him his toolbox and the list of jobs that needed doing. And if the list was too short, she puzzled until she could think of more chores, however small, to add to it. "Siege's toilet is running again," she said. "And one of the bulbs on the office sign burnt out." And Paulie said, "The least we can do, I guess, is to keep things up." And he lugged his toolbox out the door to get to his chores, and Anna realized again and again, each time with a start, that his leaving left her no more alone than his staying. She picked up his empty coffee mug and rinsed it out. She stared at the stains dyed into the bottom of the cup.

Then the talk started up about putting in a new Grand Union Shopping Plaza just down old Route 7 from the Sunset cabins. And Paulie bounded up from the dinette table in the morning, almost himself again. "You know what this means, Anna?" he asked and hugged the breath out of her. "It means Paul Bonay is on the move again, and things are looking up." And Anna laughed and washed the dishes and scrubbed the floor just like she was getting everything back to new.

Poppa Bonay died in the spring of the town planning hearings for the plaza. Anna spotted Red at the funeral. He was swaying slightly back and forth to the rhythm of the priest's Litany of the Blessed Virgin. Anna smiled at Red as she passed him on the way out of the church. Red grabbed her arm. He said he was sorry for the things he said to her when they were kids. Kids don't know any better. Anna was surprised because she didn't know Red had that kind of kindness in him. He wasn't such a bad sort after all, and she welcomed Red when he began dropping by in the evenings while Paulie attended the hearings with Dave. To keep her company, Red said. To cheer her up. It was true; Red made her laugh. He made her laugh in a way Paulie never could. She was laughing the first time Red kissed her.

Anna sees the light in Maria's cabin and smells their dinner cooking —always some stew with beans. Maria says beans are cheap and high in protein. Anna would rather eat pea gravel.

The light drains from the sky—pink and then the first hint of violet. Maybe if Red had just stayed home where he belonged, she thinks. But she relinquishes the thought half-completed, the thought she has turned round and round so many evenings like this before, because still she does not and cannot know for certain why. Still she sees Paulie's face before her, his eyes so black beneath black brows beneath that halo of blond hair. The light still burning through the darkness of his eyes like a votive candle glimmering through colored glass. "Is it true, Anna? Siege told me. You and Red. Tell me it isn't true, Anna. Say it isn't true." But he saw the truth by the fear in her eyes. And she saw the light gutter in his own. And he slammed the door that night, and she did not know until the following morning where he had gone, whether to Siege's to drink the ugliness away, or to buy a woman. She did not know until that morning when she looked up. She did not know until that second where he had gone. And then she knew. And the first thing she thought was, I'd better call the fire department to come and cut him down. But, as it turned out, she did not have to call because the arch of the post was too slender to support Paulie's weight. He was a big man. The post cracked. The body fell.

And Anna doesn't know for certain why, but she knows, she remembers what she saw in his eyes. She watched herself become what she had always been. Anna knows: we take ourselves by surprise, becoming in another's eyes what we are; we see what we already know ourselves to be. This is Anna's truth.

Construction began on Cold River Road for the Grand Union Plaza the spring after Paulie's death. Anna shops there.

The darkness sneaks up slowly. Gum wrappers and paper scraps rustle and turn with the dry leaves in the wind. Suddenly the sky drops a purple curtain. The darkness is no longer a process but a state. Stars hide in the face of it. And Anna's legs decide it's time to go inside.

As he enters the cabin, Siege trips over the pile of dirty towels. "Jesus," he says, then, "be it ever so humble. Damn Anna." Day after day, she sat out in the lawn chair picking lint off her sweater. A slob. Real trash. Some of these guys just don't have what it takes, no self respect. They don't even try to keep up. Life's a horse race, and Anna is a loser, an also-ran.

He flicks on a light, strikes a match, and lights one of the two gas burners. Thing must be an antique by now. Siege leans over the burner and lights his cigarette, then opens a can of Snow's chowder, dumps it into a saucepan. The gas flame splutters, then goes out. Damn. The bimbo let the gas run out again. Nothing works around here, nothing and nobody, he thinks. I'll grab a bite down to the Wayside.

Siege smiles at himself in the blue-tinted mirror. He stands his cigarette on its filter-tip on the burn-measled dresser top. He hunts through some hangers hooked on the bathroom doorknob for a fresh shirt.

"The clothes make the man," he says to his reflection as he buttons his shirt, red with pink lilies and curling green fronds. "Say," he says, "is that real polyester? I knew a girl named Polly Ester once, Polly Ester Blend, man-made. A real sleaze." He flips his collar up; you had to keep in step with the times.

He takes a final check in the mirror. You old dog, you, he thinks, you pup. He tousles his hair affectionately. He still had a thick head of it, yes sir. Not like poor Red. He glances out the window toward Maria's cabin. Yes sir, if he wasn't meeting Dave, he just might mosey over there and let the hot-blooded lady get lucky. Too bad about all the rug rats. Their shiny eyes unnerved him. They took everything in and gave nothing back. Sometimes he spotted the kids a nickel, a bit of spare coin. No gratitude. Kids today.

Siege picks up the butt, flicking off the silver tower of ash. "And away we go."

━━━━━━

Inside the door of the Wayside Inn (known locally and fondly as the "Wayward") Siege glances at the curling photos he's tacked there over the years. He doesn't need to look at them to see them, the Wayside in its previous incarnations: a Quonset hut stocked with military supplies during the war, the town garage full of dump trucks and road graders, then an airplane hangar for a recreational pilot, Gary Proctor, one of the marble millionaire Proctors. When Proctor tired of his latest toy, he sold the place to Siege.

Since Siege bought it, the place has housed the Moondust Ballroom, the Palms Poolroom, and the Wayside. But the Wayside today wasn't like the place in its heyday. Siege used to pack the place with his promos, baton-twirling contests and hula hoop and twist marathons. Drinking men liked to see girls, young girls. And they used to pack the place. The photos remembered. Yeah, you have to be an entrepreneur to keep a place on its feet. People want excitement. But now . . . It'd take an earthquake to shake the place out of its hillbilly cry-in-your-beer stupor. Cretin elite where the mental muffins meet. Siege shakes his head. He'd considered a disco-roller-rink-and-drink for so long that the craze rolled right on by. Just as well. Maybe a bowling alley. The place was plenty big, but you need a lot of money to build a bowling alley. The lanes alone. Siege tugs at his collar.

"Hey bartender, how's it hanging?" Siege slaps his keys on the bar. "Dave around yet?"

The bartender wipes a double shot glass on the towel tacked to the bar. "Haven't seen him," he says.

Siege glances at the kid, tries to remember his name. Where did he find these guys, anyway? he asks himself. String tie, short sleeve button-down shirt, flattop, and glasses. What a piece of work. Shit, he could play the nerd in a TV sitcom. "Anyone ever tell you you look like Clint Eastwood?" he asks.

The kid shakes his head. "Dean Martin maybe, but never Eastwood."

Siege realizes suddenly the kid isn't a kid. A man, must be in his forties at least. He snaps his fingers. "Jack," he says. That's it. "Jack."

Jack smiles. "Now you're ready for the bonus question."

"Shit," Siege says, "Jack. John. Smith. John Smith. I tell you, Jack, the easy names are the hardest to remember. The mind's the second thing to go. Heh heh. Too bad it's not the first. I tell you, Jack, I'm coming down with Alzheimer's. I'll forget my own name next. Alzheimer's. Did you see that segment on *Sixty Minutes*?"

Jack shakes his head.

"Pitiful," Siege says. "How about a brew?"

Jack brings him a Miller, wiping the condensation from the punt of the bottle.

"Christ, don't tell me you're catching it too. Morey Safer didn't say anything about the big A being contagious. I drink Rolling Rock, Jack. Always have. Always will. You know what they say—a rolling rock gathers no moss."

"It's a rolling stone, and I think it's Morley." Jack fetches the Rock.

Siege asks, "How long you been working here?"

"Oh, four or five years now, I imagine," Jack says whipping a cloth over the bar.

"Four or five years? Hell, you're a company man. Give yourself a raise." Siege slugs his beer, slips off his stool and ducks behind the bar. He punches the No Sale button, scoops out some quarters for the juke. "What am I paying you?" he asks.

"Minimum."

"No shit," Siege says. "And you'll work for that. How do I get away with it?"

Jack smiles a wide, thin smile. "Beats me."

"Yeah," Siege says. "Give yourself a raise."

Jack twists the bar cloth into a rat's tail. "How much?"

"I don't know," Siege says. "Help yourself. Whatever you deserve."

Jack shrugs. "But what do I deserve, sir?"

"Hell man. How do I know. How hard do you work? I don't know. Fifteen minutes ago I didn't even know your name."

Siege braces his hip against the juke and punches in the numbers. "Take This Job and Shove It." "My Ding-a-ling." Real class joint.

"Another beer?" Jack asks.

"Absa-tootly." "On the Road Again" blares over the speakers. "You like Willie?" Siege asks.

"Willie," Jack echoes. "Yeah sure. What's not to like. Waylon too."

"Yeah," Siege says, "Willie and Waylon. Now there's two guys who were destined to be friends. You know what I mean? Like blood. Like me and Red used to be. Did I ever tell you about the time . . ."

"No," Jack lies.

━━━━━━

When Dave opens the Wayside door, Siege is finishing up a story
Dave's heard before, many times before. Dave stands under the black-
light, and leans against a tattered poster of a unicorn. He breathes in
the smell of stale beer and urine. It took some getting used to at first.
After a while, you didn't notice it. Natural selection.

"'Drunken driving,' the officer said. So Red stands up, see. And he
said, 'No your honor, I parked the car right on the top of Razor Back
Ridge.' The judge interrupted him there, and he said, 'Tell me, Mr.
Switchel, how can you be so certain you were on the top of Razor Back
Ridge when you pulled the car off the road that evening?' And Red
said, 'Well sir, when I opened the door, two whiskey bottles fell out,
and one rolled that way, and one rolled the other.'" Siege chokes on
his laughter as he tries to finish the story. "Well, the judge had us clean
and clear. But, by God, you should have seen him laugh. He tried to
hold it in, but, Goodnight Nurse, I mean, how could you. The whole
place cracked up. But Red just stood there looking so earnest. Honest
to God, a man couldn't wish for a better guy to kick around with. What
a drinker." Siege whistles low. "A lot of fun. A wild man. I mean Dave's
okay, but Red . . ."

Siege misses the warning in Jack's eyes. "So Dave," Jack calls out,
"what'll you have?"

Dave steps forward. "Draft's fine." Dave drops a hand on Siege's
shoulder.

"Look what the cat drug in," Siege says. "Hey Godzilla, I didn't hear
you come in."

"Nice shirt, Siege," Dave says. "Hawaiian?"

"Yeah," Siege says. "It was hand woven by a couple of hula girls in a
Taiwanese factory." Siege tugs at the collar. "Think it's too subtle?"

"No sir." Dave laughs.

Siege flutters his eyelashes. "Does the red bring out my eyes?"

"Yeah," Dave says. "Liz Taylor would be jealous."

"That one's on the house, Jack, for my pal here," Siege says. "Why
don't you grab a table, Dave?"

Dave sits down. The table wobbles on one of its legs as if it were
slightly drunk. The dropped ceiling Siege installed when he converted
the Moondust to the Palms sags, cratered and pock-marked, over the
table. When Siege first set up the pool tables, customers kept bumping

the ceiling with their cues. After a while, the Ceil-Tex was so beat-up, the boys started using the tiles for a stick rack, just shoved the tips up into the ceiling where the sticks hung until they fell. There were more holes than tile now, and where there weren't holes, smudges of blue chalk dotted the ceiling. Some of the squares were so riddled with holes they hung over the tables like lace. Early Mafia, Siege called it. Dave looks around the bar. One pool table surviving, and no one was playing tonight. The men who came to the Wayside drank and drank joylessly, almost out of a sense of duty—what men like that who came to a place like this do. Women rarely came to the Wayside, never alone, occasionally on weekends when Siege hired Laughing Larry and His Sidesplitters. Sometimes as a favor to Siege, Red still came down and played his accordion. A lot of people would still come out to hear Red. Maria, once in a while, Anna, Dave himself.

Siege thumps another draft and a Rolling Rock down on Dave's table. "Criminately," he says, "sometimes I think yours truly here is a managerial genius. Honest I do. You won't believe what I've pulled on Jack. He's the bartender, you know. How sweet it is." Siege interrupts himself, "Remember that bit? 'They call me Joe,' " he sings. "Joe's bar on Jackie Gleason. That was a great bit. They call me Joe. Joe Donahee or something. Like that talk show guy's name, Dennahey, Donahue. . . . And those June Taylor dancers. Talk about a classy gimmick. That was the highlight of the week, maybe the highlight of TV. So anyway, I say to Jack, you want a raise? You decide what you're worth and adjust your salary. The guy's so rabbit-assed nervous, he can't figure out what he's worth. A dollar might be asking too much. Fifty cents, he humiliates himself. 'Bet you Abe Lincoln, the end of the week he draws his minimum wage from the till same as any other week. I'm a managerial genius, I tell you. The P. T. Barnum Bailey of the roadhouse toads. Ringmaster of the darbs. Honest to God in his F.-ing glory. A genius," he says and drinks his beer. He looks around at the tables, then at Dave, and asks, "If I'm such a genius, why isn't anybody here? It's like a cemetery in here. I'm drinking with ghosts, goddamned ghosts. Bunch of alcoholic skeletons. No flesh on their bones. Bring me some beer nuts, Jack," he yells. "*Il faut manger,* eh?" he asks Dave. "And a pickled egg," he yells.

Siege rolls the perfect oval between his thumb and forefinger, holds it too near Dave's face. "Columbus, that's me. Yeah, Columbus and the egg. A perfect world. Remember the old Moondust, Dave?"

Dave nods.

"The place full of women—not these old bums dead on their keesters. I mean flesh and blood."

Dave can smell the sulphurous brine of the egg. Siege squints his right eye studying it. "Flesh and blood," he says. He pops the egg whole into his mouth. He pounds his fist down on the table. The table lurches under the impact, spilling their beers. "Remember that, Dave, flesh—a kaleidoscope of bare arms and legs. The highlight of the week. Maybe the highlight of TV. Oh God, beautiful girls. And we had them in here, too. Remember? The flesh is willing and the will is weak. Heh-heh. Beautiful girls. Even Anna. She was a frigging piece then, a regular work of art."

Dave sits very still.

"She's a slattern now, a first class, bona fide sloven. Slattern, sloven," Siege spits. "Left a G.D. heap of dirty towels on my floor." Siege lights the filter of his cigarette.

Dave removes a folded bandanna from his shirt pocket and mops up the beer on the table. He hears Siege curse, then watches him stub the Marlboro out on the table top. He inhales the acrid smell of the burnt filter. His right hand closes over Siege's wrist. "I think you'd better get a grip on yourself," he says quietly. His grip tightens, then relaxes slowly.

"Loosen up," Siege says, and he leans over the table to peer into Dave's face. "You don't really like me; do you."

Dave looks at his uncurled hand on the table. He smiles. "You know me, Siege," he says. "I like everybody. I just like to keep things pleasant, and quiet." Dave nods toward the bar. "I think you've got a couple from the Junior League in here tonight."

Siege turns to look at the couple, then tries to focus again on Dave. "No problem, Red," he says. "I give the Liquor Control guys a case every Christmas. Before a raid, I get a call. You know what I'm saying? One hand washes the other. Plenty of time to shoo the kiddies home to bed before *Perry Mason* comes on. Dah- dah- da-da," Siege hums the theme music.

"Dave," Dave says.

"Huh?" Siege asks.

Dave smiles. "Never mind."

Siege resumes humming, then says, "Ain't I incorrigible though?" He grins and falls face forward into Dave's mug of beer.

"Just kidding," Siege says and raises his head. Foam dots his nose.

Dave hands Siege his damp bandanna. "Wipe your face, kid," he says. "Maybe you should make a trip to the little boys' room. Clean yourself up a bit."

"One hell of a baptism," Siege roars.

Dave tries to help him to his feet, but Siege pushes him off.

"Old Siege Gun can take care of himself, and don't you forget it," he says. "Dead men," he says as his hip cracks into the corner of a table. "A bunch of dead men. Dead men don't drink beer," he yells. "Lively up yourself."

When Siege returns, he carries a toilet seat.

"Boys busting up the place again?" Dave asks.

Siege stores the seat behind the bar, because rowdies kept ripping it off the john. Customers have to ask the bartender for it.

"Port-a-Potty," Siege says. He slides the seat up on his shoulder. "Howdy, podner," he says. "I'm a rootin', tootin' rustler, and I'm a-rarin' to go." He slides the seat down, raises it and pokes his head through the rim. "No, no, not the noose." He props up the lid. "Nyaah, what's up, Doc?" he asks, pointing his hands up like rabbit ears. He drops the lid again. "Awright Babalooey?" "Sawright," he answers himself.

Dave shrugs, then laughs. Some of the men at nearby tables shuffle their feet.

Siege holds the seat around his face like a frame and sings, "A pretty girl is like a malady," before switching to a nasal C-and-W twang, "You flushed me down the toilet of your heart. You tole me I warn't nothing but a fart."

Some of the men hunch together at their tables, laughing carefully.

Siege drops the toilet seat and steps into its center. "All right, ladies and germs, listen up. In this corner it's Jake La Motta. He's in the ring, and at the bell he comes out fighting." He spars with the air. "But wait." Siege slides the seat up to his knees, "Old Siege has him on the ropes. He's hog-tied. Yessirree boys."

He drops the toilet seat to the floor. "I'm hot tonight, boys. Don't want to lose my audience." He lifts the lid. "Halloo. Anybody home?

I know you're out there. I can hear you breathing." The men at the tables laugh. "Can't you see the sign, buddy?" Siege asks himself. "Men at work." Siege scratches his head. "Norton, that you? You old sewer rat you."

"Siege," Dave says, "maybe you should sit down."

"Sure, I'll take a seat," he says. He plunks the seat down on the chair and straddles it. "I'm a long, tall Texan," he sings. He slugs his beer and yanks the seat from beneath him and says, "Now we're cooking with gas, eh, Red? Ready for the musical question? 'Who wants to buy-yi-yi this diamond ring,' " he sings.

The men at the neighboring tables huddle. Some laugh, embarrassed. A few guffaw.

"What am I offered for this be-yoo-tiful ring?" Siege asks. "Who'll say one beer. Anybody. Give me one beer. I've got one beer. Who'll say two? You, that gentlegerm over there with the ears. Yeah you. I have two. Will you give me three? Make it a six-pack, and the place is yours. Believe that, and I'll sell you the Brooklyn Bridge. Going, going, gone to the soldier with the tin heart."

Dave looks warily around the bar. "Hey, easy, Siege," he says. "Down boy."

Siege holds the lid in front of his face. "I can't hear you," he says. He knocks on the lid with his right hand. "Sorry. Nobody's home." He pokes the lid out an inch. "Peek-a-boo. I see you."

Dave sinks back into his chair.

Siege flips up the lid. In an Irish brogue, he asks, "How long has it been since your last confession? Speak up, lad."

Dave ignores him. Siege repeats, "How long has it been since your last confession. Speak up. A little sin's nothing to be ashamed of."

Dave just says, "Siege," rises from his chair and walks slowly toward the bar.

"Aw, Davie doesn't want to play," Siege says to a near table. The men laugh. Humiliation, they understand. Siege holds the seat in his right hand for his new audience. "Bless me father, for I have sinned." He transfers the seat to his left hand. "How long has it been since your last confession?"

Right hand. "Three years."

Left hand. "Three years. And what are your transgressions, my son?"

Right hand. "I swore at the dog three times, father. And I drank hard liquor. And I entertained lustful notions and my neighbor's wife. And I coveted my other neighbor's wife, and his goat. But that was all one sin. And I ate sirloin tips on Good Friday, and I took Ty Cobb's name in vain. And I bore my neighbor and false witness and everyone else who crosses my path. And I killed a bottle of scotch and stole away."

Left hand. "Is there more son?"

Right hand. "Why father? Did I miss one of the commandments?"

A drinker yells, "Honor thy father and mother."

Siege rolls his eyes. "Just look at me," he says and returns to his skit.

Left hand. "For your penance say three Hail Mary's. E pluribus et dominini dominique dominique caveat canem in spiritu et gloria et cecilia et suzanna caveat emptor amen."

Right hand. "Amen."

Siege transfers the seat to his left hand, slaps down the lid and roars, "Next!" He tosses the toilet seat on the table. "Okay show's over, boys. Hey Red," he yells. No one answers. He looks around at the quiet men hulking over their tables. "Red, let's hit the road," he says, then, "Where'd that son-of-a-bitch sneak off to? You gone AWOL, Red? Damn him. How the hell am I going to get home?" He shambles toward one of the tables and thrusts his face forward, peering. "Hey, any you seen Red?" The men stare into their mugs. "Okay, any you guys seen the June Taylor dancers? May just be the highlight of Western culture." No one answers. No one laughs. Siege says, "I don't know a damn one of you. Do I? What's going on? I got to get home. Where the hell is that traitorous s.o.b.?" No one answers. No one moves. He fumbles in his pocket for his keys. "Dead men," he yells, "every one of you, but my boy Dave here. Where's Dave?"

———

"Deadbeats," he complains to Dave, as Dave drives him home. "No one's fun anymore. It's not like the good old days, eh, Red?"

"Dave," Dave says.

"I knew that. Dave," Siege says. "Shit. I left my keys in the bar."

"They're in your car," Dave says.

"My car," Siege says. "Where is it? Somebody'll steal it."

"You drove it into the ditch in the lot," Dave says. "I had to leave the keys for the tow truck."

"Oh yeah," Siege says. "That's right." He slaps his breast pocket feeling for a cigarette pack. "You got a cigarette?" Siege asks.

"Nope. 'Don't smoke," Dave says.

"Oh yeah. Right," Siege says. He slumps in the seat. His eyes squint, trying to follow the road with the headlights. His vision blurs. He closes his eyes and presses his fingertips against the lids. After a while he asks, "There weren't any cops, were there?"

"No cops," Dave says. "Jack called the tow service."

Siege thinks a minute, then says, "You're a good guy, Dave."

"Yeah," Dave says.

———————————

Dave offers to help Siege get inside the cabin.

"Shit. I can make it," Siege says. "I stand on my own two feet." He opens his door, half-falls, half-slides to the ground. He stumbles around the car and raps on the windshield. "Hey Dave," he yells, "roll down your window." He supports himself on the side of the car and leans in the window. "Me and Red, we used to be like this." He holds up two fingers for Dave to study. Dave nods. "Hey, but I don't know," Siege says. "Things change. Jesus, I feel like I been through W.W. II all over again. Did I ever tell you about the time—in the big one, W.W. II, when I led a troop of men right through the middle of an island full of Nips?"

Dave nods.

"Oh yeah," Siege says and leans more heavily against the door. "I had a good time tonight, Dave, really. Thanks." Dave watches him stumble toward his cabin. As Siege staggers down the walk, he seems to diminish until, once beyond the reach of the headlights, he disappears altogether. Dave restarts the car.

———————————

Siege trips over the pile of dirty towels when he enters the cabin. He sprawls on top of the laundry. He is still there when he wakes up in the morning.

His charm was his lack of it. He was a hard-drinking, hard-loving, fast-driving, do-nothing, good-natured son-of-a-bitch. He stumbled into every bit of trouble that could trip up a drunk's progress: scrapes with police, jilted girlfriends, irate fathers, and generous friends who found themselves shivering on cold days in hell when their loans to Red fell due. But you really couldn't fault Red. He wasn't mean or shrewd, just careless. And he didn't go looking for hearts to break, or bottles and pockets to empty. People just took to Red.

As a young man, he was good-looking with round, brown eyes that looked as guileless as a Guernsey's. A tousle of red-brown hair, the color of oak leaves turning, thatched his head. The bottle didn't disfigure Red like it did some men; it just splashed some high color in his cheeks. He stood compact, short and sturdy as a stump. He had about him the stupid, happy, surprised look of a kid who goes fishing and checks his line only to find he's hooked a trout. Women bit. And he wasn't about to throw them back. And men, admiring and envious of his ease at catching women, clapped him on the back and stood him to a few rounds at the Moondust, only to wake up in the morning with dry mouths and thinner wallets and smiles.

But the common response to Red was just to shake your head and grin. He got away with it because you let him get away with it. And you let him get away with it because he managed to do it without your much noticing at the time. There never seemed to be much expectation to the man, no intention or purpose, just a "Hey, okay. Sounds good to me" willingness to him. A carelessness people mistook for good humor. An immense recklessness.

At sixteen, it was cute. At twenty, it was no longer cute but laughable. At twenty-five, no longer laughable but still tolerable. At thirty, no longer tolerable but remediable. At thirty-five, incorrigible and pathetic. Boys who will be boys grow up into men who will be boys. Red, fortunately, broke the cycle and eventually became a man who would be a man, but at great cost—great cost.

Red was born into a lumber family with a lot of money by local standards. He grew up with nothing to do and too much money to do it with. He had expensive toys, too many of them: as a boy, Lionel trains and bicycles and scooters, and, as a young man, cars and motorcycles and women.

One of Red's expensive toys was an accordion. Red could play wonderful polkas, get people hopping just about anywhere. He was the only man around who could play honky-tonk and ragtime on the accordion. He burned the keys. Learning to play the accordion was nearly the only productive thing Red did with his life. The other was babies.

Meg Johnston was pregnant at fourteen. Red, only eighteen himself, was the father. Mr. Johnston paid both Mr. Switchels a call to suggest the younger Mr. Switchel do the right thing. No shotgun fired. Red married her less out of conscience than out of compliance. He wanted to be agreeable. He didn't love Meg, but he didn't object to her. He didn't really object to anyone or anything. He was a man at simple-minded peace with the world. If his Budweiser was in his fist, all was right with the world.

Red's father set the new couple up. They raised a clapboard building on Route 7 with a carport and gas pumps and a small mom-and-pop grocery where Red and Meg sold staples like bread, milk, and beer. In good weather, Red was usually nursing a can of the last, watching the cars whiz by, sitting on the stoop in the shade of the carport, his accordion within reach. Meg tended the register. Red pumped gas. New, the building invited passersby to stop—all white, smart with fresh paint. Meg planted red geraniums in the window boxes. Above the place, a red horse spread its wings for flight on the white, circular background of a Mobil gasoline sign. Red and Meg did a brisk business with motorists and locals.

Red's dad also set up the couple in a mobile home behind the store. The trailer, silver and stream-lined as a bullet, gleamed when it was new. Inside, the place was as efficient and clean as a factory machine. Meg had people in to dinner, and she could clean that kitchenette up with a whisk of her cloth. It was that convenient; all modern chrome. Bookshelves built into the living room and wall-to-wall throughout, and an extra bedroom for the baby.

Meg lost her first baby. Red was off drinking with Siege at the time. Red was usually off drinking with Siege. In many ways, Red and Siege were more of a couple than Red and Meg ever were. Drinking buddies, hunting buddies; they'd been pals since grade school, and they had no plans to graduate. Nearly every evening, they'd get together, split a six-pack or three, and tinker with one of Siege's old cars. "Partners in grime," Red called it. When Siege opened up the Moondust, Red became a lifer. The place became his vacation home, and he was on a long holiday. In his careless, unwitting way, Red suffered from restlessness. He wanted to be where people laughed. He didn't want to miss anything, and he didn't realize he was missing everything. Every evening, Red was at the door at opening, sometimes with Meggie, sometimes with his accordion, sometimes alone. But he was never alone for long. Sooner or later, some young lady would warm to his fatal geniality. Red was not a man to say no. Many more babies were born, none with Red's last name. And over the first decade of his marriage to Meg, Red became a one-man demolition derby. He earned the distinction of wrapping more late model cars around trees than any other man in the area, of ruining more marriages and young girls, of emptying more bottles, of walking away from the scene of the accident without a scratch on his good-natured, drunken face. But he never once raised his hand to Meg. He was not a cruel man—just reckless.

The rumors would have demolished a lesser man, a man who cared. But Red laughed them off. Meg had more trouble with the gossip. She didn't know how to laugh off the truth. She knew Red worked less and drank more. She could count the passing seasons in car wrecks—spring, Ford; summer, Dodge; fall, his father's Caddie; winter, Siege's flatbed—the way other people noted the cycle of bud to bloom, leaf to branch, frost to snow. Meg knew other women felt his weight beside them in bed. She knew babies were born and were growing up with Red's ingenuous good looks. She knew that while Red liked her well enough, his liking had not given way to love, because Red was perfectly happy with the way things were. Red was always perfectly happy with the way everything was. Why change? Why bother?

So Meg kept the trailer tidy and the grocery shelves stocked and the gas tanks full. And she took over pumping gas as Red's interest in the store declined. And she still smiled when she heard his footfall on the stoop.

Two sentences can sum up the days and years of transgression, reproach, and forgiveness. Two sentences can sum up more than a decade of their life together. Red lucked into a woman who loved him in spite of his shortcomings, one of which was his inability to recognize his good luck. Meg merely loved him. The details of their unhappiness cannot confound that truth: she loved him.

———————

The state proposed rerouting Route 7. Siege considered revamping the Moondust Ballroom as the Palms Poolroom. Meg Switchel had a baby.

Red had not understood her suffering when she miscarried. And he did not understand her joy at the birth of his son, Wayne. Red was not a man given to emotional extremes. But he liked the baby well enough. He chucked it under the chin and dandled it on his knee, and spoke of the baby's bright future before going off to suck down beers until he passed out on Siege's floor. Siege would heave him onto a cot in the Moondust office as he had a hundred times before. They were best buddies, after all.

In the mornings Siege brought Red coffee, regular with two sugars. Long after his other drinking buddies had written Red off as a loser, Siege stood by him. Long after the bartender had yelled, "Last call for alcohol. You don't have to go home, but you can't stay here," long after others had paid their tabs and fender-bended their way out of the parking lot, Siege sat on his barstool listening to Red's slurred stories loop around themselves until their narrations dwindled at last to nothing, like a logging trail in the woods. It didn't matter; Siege had heard all of Red's stories before. And he still found burping and falling on your face as funny as he had at sixteen. And if he overheard an offhand remark about Red in the bar, he cut the customer off. Siege couldn't shrug off opprobrium like Red could. And he took it upon himself to defend Red's good name with an ardor that Red couldn't muster—or understand. Red never was very good with names.

Like Anna Bonay. For years her name eluded him. He remembered her as the dump girl. When the dump girl's father died, the town chatter about it got Red to thinking about the old guy—a character with a teacher's vocabulary, the lord of the junkyard. You didn't have to check the calendar on a day you bumped into the dump man buying beer at the general store. You knew it was a payday Friday. "Thursdays were Thirst-days but Fridays were Fried-days," the cashier used to joke. Red sipped his first beer of the morning and thought, a man after my own heart. He showed up at the funeral almost sober and saw the dump girl there. The solemnity of the moment, the families of lichened headstones, the soundless sobbing of the girl, the rise and fall of Father Thibideau's mass in the foreign French and Latin, the almost frothy green of the early, still-fragile spring co-acted to create a rare moment for Red—a moment of remembrance, of realization, of remorse. He remembered teasing the dump girl as a kid. He realized her hurt. And he regretted it. But he could not remember her name. Still, he spoke to her kindly. He felt better for it. With a drunkard's sentimental sincerity, he resolved to pay the dump girl a call. He resolved to apologize. He resolved to learn her name. He was a new man of the instant, a man of integrity. He went home to celebrate with a ceremonial whiskey.

Red did learn Anna's name. And he paid a call on her to apologize and to express his condolences. His intentions were good. But his resolve had the lasting impact of a hangover. Anna welcomed him. Anna offered him a drink. And Red was not a man to say no. And one drink led to another. Bottle to body to bed to empty bottle and bed. The nights all blurred together for Red anyway. He kissed Anna. One thing led to another. Drinks, kisses, rumpled sheets to Paul Bonay, his neck snapped, dead.

Siege was home in his cabin that night. He wasn't certain what he saw. He'd been drinking. At first he thought the shape was just a shadow oddly cast by the moon, then, a kite tangled up on the sign. Then he passed out. Anna found Paulie. As local people began piecing the puzzle together, some blamed Red. They wanted to lay Paulie's death at Red's door. Others held that Red, no doubt, added to Paulie's burden, but Paul Bonay always had been a weak man. His death just proved his weakness. Anna kept to herself. Red felt bad about the way things turned out. He went on about his business. He didn't attend Paul's funeral. But he attended the next two in town.

The day of Paul Bonay's funeral, Red warmed his usual stool at the Palms. Like the good friend he was, Siege stood Red to drinks until Red no longer stood. But on that night, Red decided not to pass out in the poolroom, and he stumbled home to be in the bosom of his family where he blacked out with a lit cigarette in his hand.

That was how the fire chief reconstructed "the origins of the blaze" for the *Herald*. "A trailer acts like an oven once the pilot is lit," the fire chief explained. "Everything inside burned to a cinder in no time. Nothing could be saved. There was one survivor." One of the volunteer firemen poked his head inside the door and saw Red's feet jutting up through the smoke. They dragged him out, dead drunk. "The survivor was lying on the floor," the fire chief explained. "There's more air close to the floor, less smoke." One of the firemen gave Red mouth-to-mouth until the ambulance arrived. He revived.

———

Red no longer sells Mobil. The Pegasus sign no longer rises above Route 7. Red converted the place to a minimart convenience store a few years ago, and he sells some generic, off-price, unleaded gas. He sells sandwiches, Coke, some grocery staples. He doesn't sell beer. He no longer drinks it. He lives alone above the store. His business is one of the few out here still thriving. He's a quiet man now, and he usually keeps his own company. He still plays the accordion. The polkas still bounce. The honky-tonk rattles. But he plays his accordion only in the evening after he closes the store. It's unnerving to walk by at dusk and hear the organ strains from his apartment. Sometimes he plays at the Wayside, for old time's and Siege's sake.

I think I've gotten the story right. I've tried to be objective. But it's hard to get inside a man's skin, to think his thoughts. And even if I could get inside Red's, I don't think I'd find anything there. He's an empty man—even if the emptiness of the man today is different from his emptiness before the fire. He's burnt out. The emptiness is the terror. He has to live in it. And even if I could ask the man a question, I do not know what I would ask him. The questions I have are not for him.

The better Congregationalists around here act as if his sorrow and his sin are too gruesome for curiosity. They try to forget the past. They think the past is Red's penance; he cannot forget. They say, "Red is a good man today, a changed man." They buy bread from him. "Great suffering reforms a man," they say. They do not ask questions. They might hear the answers.

But what I ask myself, what I wonder, is: What do women see in a man like that? Meg simply, wholly loved him. But why?

It is not a question Red can answer. He has to answer his own. And I would not lie in the midnight darkness of his single bed for all the answers in the world. Restlessness of Red's sort doesn't take you anywhere. You circle round and round yourself until you drop, exhausted. You use up yourself, or you use up someone else. Red did both.

If this story is not the truth, it's as close as a man can come. I try to be objective. I try not to judge a man. I try to shut the door against my ill will. Still, now and then, a little truth sneaks in. Mostly, I try to keep out of things. I stand in the wings and watch. I'm a spectator by nature.

Like I say, I'm a spectator. Sometimes I think I see more than other people. I can open people like books, wear their eyes like a pair of reading glasses, speed-read their thoughts. Most people are easier to read than Red—just skim between the lines. Sometimes I can even catch a glimpse of myself in other people's eyes. I can tell you truths people might not even know about themselves, truths they hide from, truths they forget.

Take Siege. Siege Gun, he nicknamed himself. His real name is Timothy Taylor, a name almost remarkable for its ordinariness—like Siege himself. Siege was no war hero. All the names in the world won't change his record. Siege served all right. He served papers. He was never in the infantry—*inventory's* more like it. I learned that when a war buddy paid Siege a surprise visit one night at the Moondust. But I wouldn't blow his cover. A man's got to cling to some symbol of himself or he may find himself holding nothing at all.

I know, too, that the bartender at the Wayside's been tipping the till for years. When he needs money, he just helps himself to the register. Siege hasn't kept the books in ages. He rarely has any folding money in his pockets. Anna's been forgiving him the rent for months.

I don't dislike Siege. We're not totally unalike. He's a lonely man. Siege misses Red like a man misses his lesser half. The bottom of a bottle looks better to you when someone's sprawled beneath you. For years Red whispered like the devil on the shoulder of Siege's conscience, "Look, you can't be all wrong. I'm down here with you." Siege misses that. One day Siege stumbled into the Wayside and took a seat, and the barstool next to his was empty.

The Wayside. Or the Moondust. Or the Palms. I'm a watcher. I've watched the names come and go. But Siege is a namer, and all the names in the world couldn't elevate that place from its ashes and cigarette butts and holes in the wall. It's a dump. It's always going to be a dump. Route 7 had nothing to do with it. You could have hung out a neon sign as big as the Ritz and as glitzy and golden, and the sign would still have spelled out, "Hopeless, Hapless, and Helpless to Change It," and you would have pulled in the same crowd of gnats, Miller moths, and barflies to batter themselves senseless. Siege has the Midas touch—gold to cold.

He doesn't know treasure from trash. For all his howls about hound-dogging, he never even pet a pound puppy he didn't pay for. Harsh? Truth is harsh. I've seen him with women, crescent moons of mold rising above their eyelids, and Siege parading them like A.K.C. registered prize afghans with pedigrees. Once, I even heard Red say that if Siege ever scraped a woman's skin beneath the rouge and mascara, he'd scream in terror right there between the sheets.

Red would know. Red knew things about people in his off-hand way. He just never let the ideas become fully conscious. Instinct twice led Red to good women. You can lead a horse to water, but you cannot make him think. Red's still waiting for his first thought. But I've already told you about Red. And today, I don't know the man. But I've watched him. I've watched him until I had to turn away. I've no secrets to reveal about him, no ace in the hole. He chests his cards now.

But there are times I even feel close to Red. In the Wayside once (he was drunk, of course) he called me "Candid Camera." "You're like a lens, Dave. You take it all in, but you don't develop nothing." It almost sounded like a thought. But I'd hate to underestimate the man. I watched him. I watched him as things happened and happened to him, and he just stood there, helpless, as the film rolled on and on, helpless, as if he couldn't do anything about his life, as if he didn't have a part in it, as if he wasn't even the man he was watching on the screen.

Sometimes I thought I could feel the struggle in Red, that dreadful restlessness to go somewhere; only he was pushing both ends to the middle. Like Oliver Hardy pushing a piano upstairs, only he's also Stan Laurel pushing the upright downstairs. A man divided against himself, trying to go in two directions with a Steinway between. That's Red. And when I see him like that, that's when I feel close to him.

But I never saw the humor in Red's restlessness like Siege did. Slapstick is only funny when there is no pain. Rubber rakes are good for a laugh. Iron rakes aren't funny.

Paulie Bonay was an iron rake but rubber at the core. He was a starch and polish man. Don't-tarnish-me silverplate. He was upright like the piano between Laurel and Hardy. He was steady as Siege's drinking hand on Sunday morning. He lived for his own good opinion of himself. The man with the plan. I don't like to speak unkindly of the dead. But Bonay was the big-picture guy, the guy with the vision, Cinemascope.

He overlooked important details. And, with Bonay, you bought into his vision or you didn't. I didn't.

Bonay was a real hero. Purple heart, grazed by a bullet. He really did take an island in the Pacific—not like Siege. But Siege battles more daily with his imaginary enemies than Paulie ever did in hand-to-hand. Paulie had no real loyalty in him. He was loyal only to some notion of the hierarchy, the program. With Paulie, it was like someone peeled back the decal on his symbolism. Paulie was left with the cellophane. Siege was left with the stuff. Siege is loyal. I'll give him that. Maybe to the wrong people, the wrong things, but he's loyal, loyal and scrappy. Paulie had no fight to him. He was clean. He was efficient. He was professional. The coward coach of a group of team players.

There's a cliché; they say, "suicide's the coward's way out." I don't think it's that simple. I think the coward's way out is what takes place before the suicide. It's one thing to take your own life when you see the truth and it's unbearable. The coward blindfolds himself against the firing line of truth. That's what Paulie did.

Paulie had everything going for him—money, a good family, Anna, a nice home, a good business. When the business failed, Paulie blamed the rerouting of the road. But it wasn't the truth. Paulie lost business long before the rerouting because he had too much polish on him. The Sunset didn't do repeat business because Paulie puttered around like an old lady, so finicky, always nosing into the cabins, emptying wastebaskets, counting the towels, and making sure the kids didn't mess with anything. He couldn't let a body rest, so the business depended on motorists. No repeat trade. How can you make a go of that?

But Anna was great with the customers, not great enough to offset Paulie, but she checked people in and chitchatted with the kids. Anna would have been great with kids of her own. It's funny; none of us out here ever saw a family grow up. There's Maria's kids, but she's from away. I never married. Paulie and Anna, no kids. Red lost his boy. Siege . . . I doubt Paulie could have survived kids anyway. Paulie was too meticulous to be a survivor. I try not to judge him. I try not to judge them all. But I've felt closer to Anna and Siege, even Red, than I ever felt to Paulie. I just couldn't get next to the man.

And me? No, I don't spare the truth about myself. I didn't have kids.

I didn't fight in the war. But I learned about loneliness, and restlessness, and loyalty, and the hierarchy of power on the inside. I served time.

My crime was unspectacular, even common. The root of all evil. I worked as a foreman in a paper company, and I figured out a simple scam. I worked late. On paper I was contracting with a big trucking company, St. Johnsbury, for pickup and delivery. But actually I was contracting the work to Gypsies for about half the cost. They made late pickups and were reliable with the deliveries, and I pocketed the difference and altered the lading bills. No one was the wiser until St. Johnsbury sent a man down to learn why they'd lost our account.

Inside, you have time, all kinds of time. Time to get up, time to eat, time to dress, time to say "Yes sir" and "No sir," time to fill. You have so much time that you don't notice it's missing until you get outside.

I put my time to good use. I wrote. I read. I read anything and everything. Books about starting up your own business. Books about the movies. Books about car repair and self-improvement. Books about chair caning. And great books, too. The Bible and Twain, Fitzgerald and Faulkner, and Charles Dickens, and even Jane Austen. I read them all, one after another. I lived in them. And I read poetry, too. I wasn't particular. I'd read anything.

Inside, you learn to read and you learn to watch. You read so you can get out of your cell, go somewhere else for a while. And you watch because you have to. You have to know what's up, who's who. You have to choose your friends carefully, and you have to be loyal to your friends, or you find yourself with no one covering your back. And you learn to respect men for whom you have no respect, because they jangle the keys on the ring, and they keep the files in the warden's office. They think they know you in black and white. It all comes down to the fine print.

And my fine print was fine and clean. And my day rolled around. And I was released, and the eight years I served were released on the same day. I never saw them again.

I had my money tucked away. She was still waiting for me like a loyal wife. I decided not to go home, to put some distance between me and the past. Beyond that, I didn't have a plan. First off, I bought a car, a shiny, red convertible. I wanted air and space. And I let that car drive like it had a brain under its hood instead of an engine. I let it take me. And it took me up Route 7, and I saw all the new businesses going up.

As clean as modern progress, as clean as the wax shine on the hood. I took control of that car, and I pulled over—not so far from home after all.

When I first got out of prison, I couldn't read. The book covers weighed heavy in my hands, heavy as time. But I loved movies. I used to park in whatever downtown I was cruising through at the time and locate the Strand or the Bijou or whatever the local movie house was called, and I'd huddle into the dark, popcorn crunching beneath my soles, and I'd watch the plots unreel, the stories flicker to the last frame. But I hated the closeness, the pestering flashlights of the ushers, some kid spilling Nehi and kicking the back of my seat, the wheezing of some body hulking next to mine, elbows battling for the armrest.

And as I sat on the side of Route 7 looking over the flat floodplain to the river, it hit me. A drive-in.

It was beautiful. A candy-striped playground for the kids. A concession. Double features on Friday night. The teenagers smuggling friends in their car trunks while I looked the other way. The cartoons flickering at dusk. Sleepy children in their pajamas swinging back and forth. Laughing. Crying. Overeager teens steaming up the rearview windows while dancing hot dogs and hamburger buns sang, "Let's go out to the lobby. Let's go out to the lobby." And at last the cries and laughs and the darkness settled. The stars popped into place. And the car doors slammed, and the kids fell asleep in the piles of pillows and blankets in the back of the station wagon. And Mom and Dad nestled together in the front seat sharing popcorn and Milk Duds. The feature glimmered onto the screen, and kids from the development on Cold River Road climbed the fences for a stolen peek. Dave's Twilight Drive-In.

Nothing had ever felt so right to me. Night after summer night, I packed the lot with cars. I showed the great old movies. Astaire and Rogers; Garland; Davis in *Hush . . . Hush Sweet Charlotte; The Wizard of Oz* for the kids. But my favorite, along with most of the rest of the world, was and is *Gone With the Wind*.

I can close my eyes and see Clark Gable say to Vivien Leigh, "Frankly, my dear, I don't give a damn." And I see her face, I see her realization that the past has finally come home, that this is the culmination of all her past actions, all the frames of the film—that he is gone. And it is too late to change that. She has gone too far in the direction she's been trying to push him all along. She pushes too hard. One nudge too much. She succeeds at last, and she fails. And I see the momentary helplessness—almost triumphant—in her face. At last, something, someone is beyond her control. There is nothing left to do but go on. Alone.

The Civil War is almost incidental. It is a great love epic, the greatest. And sometimes I try to imagine Sherman and Lee and Grant in the audience watching themselves and their history relegated to walk-on roles as Gable and Leigh transcend history and the screen, their love looming large over the trivia of war—the countless dead and wounded, Atlanta burning a way of life to the ground. Stars can do that.

In my daydreams I used to imagine myself with star quality, scooping up the woman I loved and carrying her up the stairs. But I'm no Gable, no actor. I'm just a watcher.

Sometimes when I watch that movie, I wish I could reach in and change events, tell Scarlet to snap out of it, and Rhett to give a damn, and Melanie that she's too good for that petri dish of agar, mold-growing Ashley. But the characters in movies are who they are. Even if you could intervene, you wouldn't, because then they would not become who you already know them to be. The movie has a will of its own.

I remember once being in the projection room, watching a film unreel. It had unthreaded from the take-up reel somehow, and it fluttered away from the projector, wound and unwound on the floor. The projectionist was in the men's room. Cars below beeped their horns. People shouted. And I stared at the film coiling and uncoiling on the floor, tangling into a knot of celluloid that felt like it was in the pit of my stomach. But I didn't know how to stop it. I was helpless. I feel exactly the same way when everything goes perfectly and I watch the movie. My will is meaningless. My muscles run to water. I can only sit and watch. The movie runs on and on. I watch.

I'm the champion watcher. I've watched the people in this neighborhood set methodically about the business of wasting their lives. And I watched the new plaza go up on Cold River Road. And I watched the new Cinema Five go up with its five minitheaters. And I watched the crowds dwindle at Dave's Twilight Drive-In. I watched the weeds grow up in the parking lot, and the candy stripes rust on the swing set, and the paint peel off the concession stand, and the wires on the speaker boxes snap. I watched until I saw. I see the truth, but I try not to blame.

The truth is harsh enough without the burden of my judgment. The truth is its own judgment. And the truth is that I didn't see the change coming anymore than Anna saw Paulie's weakness, or Siege saw Red's moral meagerness, or Red saw time and the bottle running finally dry. But the change came, putting along like a gasoline-conserving compact car. And the people stopped coming. And the business started to go under until, now, the only way I can keep going is by showing sleazy movies to horny farmboys. *Deep Throat* would be a class feature on my marquee. I can't bear to watch the plotless junk. Those aren't movies. They're marital aids for men with inflatable wives. And even that isn't disgusting. It's merely sad, merely lonely. It's the truth, and I try not to judge it.

In prison, I read in Matthew: "Judge not, that ye be not judged. For with what judgment ye judge, ye shall be judged." The words resounded in my cell with truth. I resolved from that day on I would never cast the first stone. I withdrew from judgment, and I tried to live out my life according to that truth, to be a watcher but not a judger.

But something went wrong. I stood aside. I knew my own sins and the sins of others. I saw them all. But I kept my mind clear, my judgment clean, oh yes, as clean as Pilate's hands. And there's the greater sin—my perfect sin of omission. I mistook passivity for forgiveness, impassivity for mercy, inertia for virtue. I stood by and I did not judge. I stood by and said, "See YOU to it." And I watched Paulie hang himself. I watched Red's family die. I watched Anna doom her life. And in each case there were moments—pure, isolated moments—when I could have stepped in, interrupted the momentum toward these ends. I could have helped Paulie along; I had some money then. I could have asked Siege to cut Red off at the bar, said, "Your pal is drinking himself or somebody to death." I could have gone to Meg and said, "He's no good to you like that. Lock the door against him." I could have warned Anna against Red, because I saw everything happening. I saw everything moving toward its inevitable conclusion. There were moments. I watched them pass. I do not know why.

Because I did not want to get my hands dirty? Because I did not want to meddle? Because I did not choose to judge? Because, after all, I am what I am, and I am suited for nothing in life but to watch it roll by. Like Red, I live with myself.

I still see things around here. I notice and take note. I watch as everything changes, and I stay the same. The years I lost in prison arrested time for me. I'm like a rerun on TV. I'm a clock without hands. I'm fixed in time even as it ticks along. Anna, Paulie, Siege, Red, Meg— I watched them all. I even watched myself watching myself. A waste. Endless.

And sometimes I have even watched and seen nothing. Like Maria. I've watched her for years. I've watched her come and go. I've watched her scolding the kids in the words I cannot understand. I've watched her. But I cannot see her. Some hearts you cannot penetrate.

So I write this. I'm just trying to make some sense.

Maria sits on the bed and counts out her change. She counts it out more carefully than usual, fondling each coin, listening to the clink of the dimes, the clunks of the quarters and nickels. Cassie would be closing the stand soon, and Maria wouldn't have the extra money.

The children tumble in the corners, under the bed, stalking each other, pouncing from the shadows. They play at cats. A hand claws Maria's shoe off her foot. Dark eyes glint at her from the bathroom door. "Mama meow," Pepe says and hisses. The shadows in the room giggle.

"I told you to hush," Maria says and kicks off her other shoe. The shadows scrabble under the bed.

Maria loses count. She begins again, building the coins into silver towers with copper rims. She remembers when she first saw Cassie and Gene's roadside stand. August. Armfuls of gladiolas upright in buckets along the road—the brilliant reds and pinks, the whites so bright in the sun they looked silver. The colors of her homesickness, the colors of home.

In the summer, Cassie sold flowers and produce, flats of pansies and Johnny-jump-ups, baskets of summer squash and cucumbers, bins of peas and corn. This time of year Cassie tempted the tourists and leaf-peepers off new Route 7 with cider and apples, pumpkins, and her homemade doughnuts.

The farm has belonged to Gene's family for six generations. "The people keep coming back," Cassie says, "year after year. They remember us."

Cassie doesn't worry about the farm. Her father-in-law paid off the mortgage decades ago. She works it. Gene works it. Other farms in the area have faltered, gone under. The land's become too valuable to farm. A developer from Mountain Men Real Estate Management and Development, Inc., offered Cassie and Gene a nice sum for the spread. He wanted to build condos for the overflow of ski-people from the mountain.

"You guys don't get it, do you?" he argued. "If you don't come to the mountain, soon the mountain will come to you. The development's heading this way. You might as well try to sandbag yourself against a flood with beanbags. You're going to be engulfed anyway. A smart person could make oceans of money."

Cassie plopped some ripe tomatoes into a paper sack. "Not interested," she said.

"I'm telling you," the Mountain Man said, "your stone walls will not fence McDonalds and the malls out. You're going to be surrounded."

Cassie handed him the sack of tomatoes. "No charge," she said. "And no sale."

After the man left, Maria asked, "Why did you give him the tomatoes for nothing?"

Cassie smiled. "One of them was wormy."

When Maria walked back to the Sunset that night, she spotted the bag on the shoulder of the road. At first she thought it was a dead animal, but, as she neared, she could see the tomatoes split, spilling their seedy pulp onto the road, blotting the ragged paper bag with watery red stains, and, nearer still, the ants crawling over the red mash. She smiled. Perhaps the Mountain Man had bitten into the worm? More likely he threw the tomatoes out untasted.

Maria admired Cassie and Gene. They did okay for themselves. They got by and got on. Not like the other losers around here. The place was lousy with losers, crawling with losers.

Tiny fingernails scratch her calf. A run ladders the leg of her pantyhose. She thrashes at the unseen hand with her foot. "Great," she yells. "Who is that? Is you, Carlos? Pepe? Otto. Come out. That's two dollars. Two dollars and twenty-nine cents. You kids think we're made of money. Now what do I wear to work tomorrow?" Her hand slashes under the bed, snags a collar. She tugs Carlos out by the scruff. "See what you done," she says.

The dark eyes catch the light. *"Lo siento, Mama."*

"Speak English," she snaps. "You're American now."

Eyes blink at her around the room. Sometimes when she scolds them, she lapses into Spanish herself. She studies Carlos. *Pobrecito.*

"Come here, all of you," she says. Her arms are not long enough to surround them. Sometimes she thinks she has lost count of her children. "Carlos, you be more careful. You are the biggest; you have to be good. Get the mattress now."

Carlos unrolls the mattress from the closet.

When they are sleeping, curled against each other, their breaths like purrs, she can count them. Four dark crowns of hair. Eight hands. Eight feet. Forty fingers. Forty toes. All boys. Carlos. Pepe. Otto. They call the youngest Nene, but his name is José.

When they first came over, she worried about their names, their foreignness. But she did not change them. You had to save something from the past.

She looks at the sleeping children and drapes the blanket over their tangle of bodies. By daylight, they seemed to multiply like stray cats, a litter of wild kittens ripping up her nerves. But at night, calm and tame as drowsy lap cats, they settled into their dreams. They were all in school now—even Nene. Playschool in the morning. Daycare at the "Y" in the afternoon. Her life would be easier now.

In school, they learned English and French. Too many languages, Maria thought. But she is happy they are in school. Things are better here than they were at home.

Carlos murmurs in his sleep, and she kneels by him and smoothes his hair out of his eyes. Carlos most resembles his father. He wears his name. But Maria hopes he will not be afraid like his father, skittish as some garden sparrow eyeing Cassie's scarecat. But she thinks young Carlos is too scrappy to be afraid. He's an alley cat, a tom.

His father was like that when Maria first met him—a tom, on the prowl. But after they married, Carlos grew fat and lazy. They married two months before young Carlos was born. His father got him a job as a surveyor with a company in San Juan. But he moved too slow setting up the tripod. He was careless with the transit and tape. The sun tired him, he said, made him feel drunk. After he was fired as a surveyor, he found other jobs. Never for too long.

Maria got a job at Multi-Media when Carlos was fired the first time. Multi-Media offered daycare to its employees. Maria worked in the mailroom. Multi-Media was a big corporation, its headquarters rooted in America. It had many branches. That was how Maria came to America. She wanted Carlos to come. But he was afraid. Too cold, he said. Too far away. Carlos did not speak English. Mama's boy, she said, and she came over alone with the children. Sometimes they sent Carlos postcards. The kids would paste sticker stamps on the postcard.

The older boys signed their own names, their signatures sprawling over the card. Maria had little room left over for her words.

Carlos wrote to her once in English that he was taking a class—ESL, he wrote. And when he could speak good, he would come to her and the boys in America. But he did not write again in English. Maria's mother wrote that Carlos was no good, always at the beach sitting in the sun with the American girls. Maria wondered if maybe now he could speak English. But she didn't really care any longer. She made the boys write him because he was their father. But she knew, if you wanted to get ahead, you had to drop whatever baggage was slowing you down. Carlos was excess baggage.

Maria learned English at Multi-Media. They also offered language classes to their employees. She saved her money and applied for a transfer, and they sent her here. Now she was saving money again so she could move out of the cabin, rent one of those new apartments in the townhouse development on Cold River Road where the boys could have their own room, and she could have a kitchen instead of a hotplate and refrigerator.

She kisses Carlos on the forehead. She tucks the blanket under the corner of the mattress.

Maria also wanted to move out of the mailroom at Multi-Media, so she worked hard, the early morning shift. Winter would come soon and Cassie would close the stand. In the winter, Cassie sold maple syrup, but she sold it from the kitchen, not the stand. She hung out a sign on the roadside and people knocked right on the kitchen door. Maria thought it would be nice to work at home. With Cassie's stand closed, she would need another job for grocery money. No work around here, that was certain.

She pads in her stocking feet to the bathroom. She steps out of her clothes and slides on the robe hanging on the door hook. The robe smells musty, the smell of the bathroom, the smell of mildew. The halo of fluorescent light spits and hisses. Her skin appears green in the light. She splashes water on her face. She looks forward to this time of night.

She will slip on her scuffs and lie on the bed and plan. She has planned so often that sometimes the plan dances behind her eyes like a dream, shadowy like an old film, uncertain, shuddering over splices. In the plan, Carol, her boss, retires. Carol is old and tired and has corns on her toes. She wears nurse's shoes to work to ease her feet. She snaps at the girls, then apologizes. She says it is just her change of life. All of Carol's kids are out of college now. Carol will not stay at Multi-Media much longer. Behind her back, the girls snicker at her. They wait for her to leave.

Then Maria becomes supervisor like Carol. Only the girls *like* her because she is one of them with kids at home, jokes in the lunch room, polish on her fingernails, no corns on her feet. They will like her and work hard for her so her figures are good and she gets a raise. Then she can save more money, and they will move into the townhouse and buy a new car, and the boys will go to college, so they can make money. They will start at the top.

But sometimes Maria hears snickers at the edges of the plan. Sometimes she thinks she hears the girls laughing after she leaves the lunch room, after she mispronounces a word. Once the girls were talking about the upcoming long weekend, Lincoln's birthday. "Hey Maria, I bet you don't even know why we get the day off," Debbie, one of the sorters, challenged her. "Oh I know," Maria said. "Is the day Mr. Lincoln fred the slaves." And the girls laughed out loud; "fred," they kept repeating, laughing again. Only Carol did not laugh. "Freed," she said. "Freed," Maria repeated, but the laughter confused her. She may have said "fred" again. She wasn't sure. She tried to laugh along. The girls liked jokes.

Maria lies on the bed and tries to outline the plan. But the plan blurs. She knows it is there. She knows the words, but they write themselves out in the strange alphabet of a foreign language. She cannot decipher them. When she cannot read the plan, she buys a lottery ticket in the grocery store—just in case. She doesn't buy them too often, though, because the lottery is for losers.

Like Siege in number four. Siege buys a lottery ticket every day. When they cross by each other on the concrete pad of the courtyard, Siege sometimes stops her. "When my ship comes in," he says, "I will take you away on a cruise." Maria smiles, but she knows his ship sank years ago. Siege is a loser. She wouldn't board a ship with him. She wouldn't cross the street with him. She doubts he knows how to sail a ship anyway.

They are all losers here. Siege, an old man, drunk and dressed out like a color-blind San Juan pimp. And the big man, Dave. He looks kind but sad, shambling around Anna like a circus bear on a short chain who doesn't realize he could snap it with one little tug. He always looks like he is sorry for being where he is, sorry for being in his skin. He hangs around Anna making excuses. He is in love with Anna. Maria sees it in the way he crunches his hat in his big hand. A grown man and he acts like a boy in a sideshow who has never seen a woman before. Anna is deaf to the words heavy on his tongue. Anna does not hear the love in his apologetic silences. But that is just as well.

Anna has enough trouble. Anna is also kind, but she lives in some other place. She never lives wholly here. She looks like a heap of unsorted clothes in a Salvation Army bin. She sits out in her lawn chair long after the sky turns cold. She sits and picks lint off her sweater. She is very kind, but she lives in her own mind.

When Maria moved into the cabin, Anna brought her a bouquet of purple gladiolas. "I thought the place might be able to use some color," Anna said. Maria thanked her. She put the gladiolas in a plastic pitcher on top of the blonde dresser. The gladiolas were rich and purple as midnight. They could not brighten the cabin.

And Red, the accordion man, the man at the little grocery. He was doing okay. He didn't look like a loser, but he was. He sold lottery tickets, but Maria did not buy hers there. They said he was bad luck. She bought gas there, though, for her salt-eaten, green Datsun. He pumped the gas. In summer, he wore sunglasses. Someday Maria would buy a new car.

She pulls the blankets higher up her chest. She feels the winter cutting into the air, but she does not want to use the heat too early. She does not want to get too comfortable before the real winter comes. She would save her money. Money was insurance against becoming a loser.

Cassie and Gene were not losers. Gene still milked all year long although they closed the dairy on the farm. Gene sold his milk to a big company dairy now. Maria wonders how Cassie and Gene have managed to keep the machinery working, the fields and the cows productive, the produce stand full, how they managed to keep turning their life to gain. "What's your secret?" she asked Cassie as they peeled back the husks on ears of corn, checking for signs of worms.

"No secret," Cassie said. "It's hard work each day as it comes and don't look too far ahead or you'll get discouraged."

"Why do you keep apart from the other people out here?" Maria asked.

"Never got to know them," Cassie said.

"Why not?" Maria asked.

"We're busy. And they came after us," Cassie said. "We're older than they are. We're farmers. I expect they look down on us."

But Maria thinks it's more than what Cassie told her. Cassie is connected. To the farm. To Gene. Maria can feel the connectedness. She would like to feel connected. She has the children, but they are connected to her. She would like to bring her mother over, save up money after she moves into the townhouse apartment, and bring her mother over on the plane. She adds it to the plan.

A knock on the door startles her. She glances at the children. Maybe the man Siege is drunk again. She lies still and doesn't answer the door. Knock again. Then a face wavers in the window. The ghost opens its mouth. "It's me, Maria. Anna," the face mouths at the glass.

Maria rises. Three strides toward the door. "Mrs. Bonay," she says. It sounds like a question.

Anna hands her a plate of cookies. Eight, Maria counts them.

"I saw the light on," Anna says. "I thought the children might like them. They're cookies."

"They're asleep," Maria says and glances again at the mattress on the floor.

Anna looks at the eight cookies on the plate. She moves her thumb, covering a chip on the plate's rim. "Maybe I should have brought more," she says. "They're nothing special. Storebought. I got them at Red's. Oreos," she adds. It sounds like an apology. Anna stares at the plate still in her hand.

Maria tightens the sash of her robe and pokes the screen door ajar with her foot. Her hand reaches for the plate. "Thank you," she says. "I'll save them for tomorrow."

The light settles softly on Anna's face. She looks slightly bewildered, younger by this light. Her face is uncertain, expectant. Its beauty surprises Maria. "You would like to come in?" Maria asks.

"Oh, oh no," Anna says, and her face pulls back from the shaft of light. The darkness sifts into the familiar network of wrinkles and creases that Maria recognizes as Anna's face. "I wouldn't want to disturb the children," Anna says.

Maria nods.

Anna recedes into the darkness. Maria listens to the dry leaves crunch beneath her feet.

Maria places the plate of cookies on the nightstand and climbs back into bed. She picks up an Oreo and twists the discs of chocolate, licks off the white cream, then presses the chocolate halves back together and replaces it on the plate. While the filling dissolves in her mouth, she reviews the plan. She arranges herself for sleep, arranges the plan in her mind so she will dream it. She falls asleep with the light on. This is what she dreams:

It is morning. The first frost ices the stubbled grass of the courtyard. The boys laugh and jabber in excitement. A new car is parked in the circular driveway. Sometimes it is a Trans-Am. Sometimes it is a minivan, a Voyager. But it is always red and shiny. The boys clamber into the car. "It is as red as a fire engine," Carlos shouts. The vanity license plate says, "WIN" or "RUN." She cannot make it out. The letters quiver, oscillate, transmute themselves. The boys' arms and hands wave from the windows of the van, flutter like leaves on windy branches. In the back seat, the children perch on piles of pumpkins and grapes, heaps of apples and pears. Long stalks of ripe corn protrude from the windows. Their tassles unfurl like pennants. Maria effortlessly tosses the luggage—the suitcases bursting their locks, the boxes of broken toys and battered Golden Books—onto the roof rack.

Anna and Dave and Siege stand arm-in-arm with another man and woman, unfamiliar to her, in a semicircle around the busted post in the courtyard. Maria swishes by them in the watery rush of her red silk dress brushing against her stockinged thighs. A halo of red gladiolas crowns her black hair. She brushes grapes and cherries from the bucket seat and slides behind the driver's wheel. The van snorts to life. The children cling to the corn stalks, the tassels like streaks of blonde in their hair.

"Adios, you losers," Maria shouts. The tires squeal with delight. They're singing down the road.

She dreams in Spanish.

"Boy, did we make a wrong turn," the man in the red Trans-Am says.

"We?" she says. "You." She spins the gold bracelet on her wrist, flips down the vanity mirror and applies lipstick expertly to her lips. She smacks her lips together. "Well, get us out of here," she says. "We're running late as it is."

"Turn down the damn music," he yells. He rustles a map, jabs it with his index finger.

She taps her foot either to the Bruce Springsteen tape or to the rhythm of her own impatience. "It's a time-share," she says, "time-share." She points at her Rolex for emphasis. "We've only got the weekend. If you wait until April to find your way out of here, the snow will all be gone. I'm not about to sit here 'til next spring."

"I told you to turn down the music," he yells again. He unrolls his window and sticks his head out, scouting for some marker to locate him.

"Why don't you go into that office and ask directions," she suggests.

He looks up at the run-down office building, the dilapidated cabins. "Yeah, for sure," he says. "You'd love that. Norman Bates's mother could give me directions to the local morgue."

He shakes the map out, hitting the Playboy Club memento dangling from the mirror. The bow-tied rabbit swings back and forth almost in time to the music.

"I've got it," he says. "This isn't Route 7. We're on Alternate 7. See?" He bends the map back for her.

She looks in the mirror. "Well then let's get the hell back on Route 7. Why don't you watch where you're going?"

"Maybe you'd rather walk," he says.

She flips the visor up.

The red Trans-Am cuts across the road, U-turns, whips back along Alternate Route 7.

It is mud season along old Route 7. The cabin courtyard runs with marshy water beneath the snow. A few salt-filmed cars nose around the gas pumps at the minimart. A pick-up spins its tires in the Wayside parking lot, splattering mud, sinking deeper and deeper, hoping at last to strike something solid, bedrock, and rear up out of the mud. The engine whines. Steam rises from the heat of the hood in the cold air. Muddy snow banks against the sign in front of the Twilight Drive-In. "See you in the sprin," the sign reads, the "g" obliterated by a crusty drift of snow. Beyond the vegetable stand, the furrows of the field dip into troughs of wet snow from the thin ridges of mud.

No one is in sight. No one stands along the road to see a red Trans-Am streak down old Route 7. No one hears the crescendo-decrescendo from the window of the passing car. A flash of music—two full bars— the tempo distorted by the speed of the car, by the instant it outraces— unidentifiable even if someone were there to hear it. But no one is.

The land lies fallow. The land lies still. The land sleeps beneath the snow waiting for spring. The land does not know that in the chalet-style office building of Mountain Men Real Estate Management and Development, Inc., a man has big plans for the land. "Level land, good drainage, great commercial potential, and cheap," the man thinks as he taps a pencil eraser against the lucite top of the desk. "Very cheap. Those old businesses will leap at the chance to sell out. Dirt cheap."

He writes himself a memo. He is as determined as a bulldozer. He has big plans for the land. Big plans. Big dreams.

CAMP ▊

I'M WATCHING MY SON Toby swim, hands walking the sand bottom, in the lake where my mother watched me groping bottom when I was Toby's age. A girl flippers by Toby, then drifts facedown, hands extended in a dead man's float. Her red suit bubbles with air. Toby thrashes, chuckling, oblivious to the troubles that deposit us here. Healdville, Vermont, my bottomland.

The first time the bottom fell out of my life, I also landed here, but Toby wasn't born yet. That was my first failed marriage. No children. Divorce stories are the war stories of peacetime; everyone has one, and no one wants to listen to it. Now I have two no one wants to hear.

The girl in the red bathing suit stands, twists her sunstruck yellow hair, wringing lake water down her neck. She grins at Toby, her mouth pointy with arrowhead teeth.

"Boy, hey boy," she says, "I can swim all the way to the raft by myself."

Toby ignores her. "Look, Mom," he calls, waddling on his hands, "I'm swimming."

I flash the thumbs-up sign. Near the shore, a perch glints and shudders, disappearing beneath the shadow gliding over my shoulder and across the green water. I squint up.

"Beautiful day."

"Hmmm," I say. I push the nosepiece of my glasses, darkening the image against the haloed sun so I can make him out. Stranger. The man who must be the girl's father smiles down into my Ray-Bans. He's handsome in an ordinary way, brown hair, curly and gray-wisped, straight nose, a cute little middle-aged paunch he's sucking in for the first impression, but he has the eager look of the marriage veteran, another one who's jammed one too many milk bottles into the grocery carton only to have a bottle break through the soggy cardboard bottom. Crash and splat. He flaps his towel and plops down next to me. "Great place for kids," he opens.

As he flops down—a blur of kelly green swim trunks, a mat of chest hair—I think of tucking in my stomach, too, but the moment of vanity passes. I'm just not interested. Not that I dislike men, I just don't like the way I act when I am with them, how my cutesiness during courtship makes me feel like a smiley face sticker that curls off as the adhesive dries during the habituation period when you learn that he snips his toenails off into the toilet and he learns that you get claustrophobic sharing the clothes closet—too many hangers for one pole.

He crooks his arm, props up his head. "You staying here for the summer?"

"Don't know," I say. "Transition. I'm biding time at my Mom's." I rustle the *Rutland Herald* in my lap.

"Oh," he says, "I'm in transition, too."

As he burbles on, I regret my mistake.

"Divorce," he says. "It's no day at the beach." He brays at his unintended pun. "Haw-haw. I'm renting the cabin over there. My wife, my ex, she lives over in Fair Haven. I wanted to be close to Rachel, my daughter. It's tough."

I can't bear another undressing of the wounds.

"Well, life is tough." One platitude to mercy-kill another. I unfold from my beach chair and splash out to join Toby. The water slides gooseflesh cold over my calves and thighs. Rachel, the red-suited, spins, her hair an eddy on the green water.

"Rachel, hey Rache," her father calls in a false, overly hearty voice. "Does my mermaid want to swim out to the raft?" He stands and adjusts his waistband below his navel. He's loving his body, tensing his muscles with a self-consciousness that yells, "Look at me," like Toby shouts when he belly flops into one of his knee-deep dives. I shift my eyes behind my sunglasses, annoyed with the man's play for attention, stoop and slide my hands around Toby's fishy middle. He giggles as I lift him to a float. "I'm swimming. I'm really swimming." His flutter kick splashes prisms into blue air, streaks onto my dark glasses, beats in my heart. I love him so much. My hands fumble to hang on to his slick eel's body.

I learned to swim here. In the summer, my mother would walk down the dirt road, my brother, Paul, and I tumbling ahead of her, scouting tiny toads, whipping each other on with cat-o'-nine-tails grabbed from the shallows, shrieking as we scrambled to the beach. Paul learned the crawl before I did, but I learned to backfloat first. "You simply relax. Hold still," Mom would say as she'd balance him in the water. And over and over, as she slid her supporting hands from him, he'd drop sudden as a sinker, only to splutter back to the surface and my laughter as I lay, arms outstretched and eyes open to the wide July sky, floating with the current.

My mother still lives in the red house where we grew up. I still call it the red house although she painted it white after my dad died. Toby sleeps in Paul's old room, his toys still lining the shelves as if expecting his imminent return, but Toby plays with the steel trucks and wood blocks now. Paul lives in California and rarely comes east.

Red Rachel thrashes near Toby, her palm slicing through the water ahead of her nose like a dorsal fin. "Dah-dah, dah-dah, dah-dah," she chants the ominous movie theme. Feeding frenzy. As she snaps, Toby chuckles. I release him to dog-paddle to the girl. I splash my way to the hard band of sand and resume my place in the sun.

Rachel's father looses his drawstring, adjusts his trunks lower on his hips, splashes water on his forearms and his legs before diving in. He surfaces and shakes the water from his hair. "Rachel, I'm going to get some exercise. Don't go out over your head." And he's off, stroking across the lake toward the island.

When Paul and I were young, we used to take the canoe out there, step onto the spongy bushy ground, releasing a startle of birds into the air. The world was an adventure then, an invitation to a mystery. We thought life was a riddle invented for us to solve, and like two detectives we determined to solve it together until the summer of the crab apple wars when Paul became secretive and everything changed.

The summer Paul turned thirteen, I turned eleven, two years and two days apart, both June birthdays falling just after school let out with a whoop and a whistle. Although we didn't know it then, it was also the first summer of Dad's sickness. We knew that he was gray, that he slept downstairs, the parlor converted to a bedroom. He slept more than usual and read, the shades drawn against the light. My mother tried to conceal from us the sadness my father was too steeped in to conceal. We'd peek in and find him, head tilted against the trellised wallpaper, book fanned open to a page that never turned. "Hey kids," he'd call. "I'm just reading." But the room, the umber light, his linty pajamas, the unread book smelled so strongly of illness that we were too afraid to mention it.

Instead, Paul and I poked around as we always had, catching tadpoles, playing tag in the Civil War cemetery, finding spitworms on the devil's paintbrushes, canoeing around the island, shooting BBs into the tin cans at the dump. But in early July, Paul started hanging out with Den. At fourteen, Denny Dorman, the shopkeeper's son, was one of the big kids. He and some of the other teenaged boys used to sun themselves at the lake, stirring occasionally to throw one of the prettier protesting teenaged girls off the diving board.

As Paul spent more time with Den, I turned my attention to Linda White, whose mother raised Morgan horses on the mountain road. Linda had some other girlfriends who came over to ride, and we all buddied up for slumber parties and birthday parties, for which occasions Mrs. White would loan one of her horses and lead the girls around the corral advising them how to sit, point their feet, how to post.

As a group, we began rowing out for picnics in *Miss Tipsy,* the Whites' dinghy. We'd pick water lilies and trail their snaky stems lazily through the water as we giggled and dreamed aloud about who we'd get for a teacher next year, who we'd like to become, who we'd like to marry. Some days we drifted out to the island and tossed crusts torn from our cucumber or egg sandwiches for the birds who swooped by circumspectly before pecking. But sometimes the fish would nip the crumbs off from below just as perplexed starlings and swallows beaked the water's surface. We might have drifted indolent and undisturbed through that summer, but then Paul began getting into trouble.

One July night, Mr. Dorman knocked on our door and accused Paul of stealing *Playboy* magazines from the rack at the store. While they talked, Paul bounced his weight from the ball of one foot to the other. I fiddled with the strap of my bathing suit, which cut into my neck, shrinking as it dried. When Mr. Dorman left, my mother sent me to my room, but I listened through the heating grate in the floor as she confronted Paul.

"No," Paul said repeatedly. "No. Den took them. And it's his father's store. He can't steal from his own store."

My mother murmured for a while, a mother's sermon. I recognized the rise and fall, the rhythms, but the only words I caught clearly were: I don't want you hanging out with Dennis Dorman. People judge you by the company you keep.

But I knew Paul was still palling around with Den. I'd see them dumping pails of water on the girls suntanning on the beach, or I'd spot them fishing from the Dormans' rowboat near the spillway, hooting as the red and white floats bobbed, snapping up a trout or perch.

The following Sunday, Paul got into trouble again. Les White, who mowed the school grounds during the summer, had gone up and found the cafeteria window soaped with swear words, many of them misspelled, he said. Gossip pointed to Denny and Paul. Again, Paul insisted on his innocence to my mother as she warned him off the Dorman boy. As I stood watching them, my mother wagged her finger, threatening, "This time I mean it. I'm telling your father." Paul stared at her; she stared at him, fear reflected in his eyes and hers, fear and the unspoken knowledge that the source of it was not that she would tell our father, but that she wouldn't. She was afraid to tell him. The invocation of my father no longer summoned a respectful attack of watery legs and quavery voice but an image of a listless man propped up against the corner of the parlor wall, forgetting to turn a page as he immersed himself in some more solitary and singular reading. My mother and Paul held each other in the spell of their fear until Paul broke it, dropping his eyes, saying, "I didn't do it."

"You shouldn't be hanging out with vandals. I told you, you'd be judged by the company you keep. The hoodlum can't even spell."

"Denny isn't a hoodlum, and he, and we didn't do it. I swear."

My mother scoffed at the word *swear*. But she'd run out of words. What more could she say? She had no proof. But witnesses could verify the snapping turtle incident.

On the far side of the lake where they'd been fishing, Den and Paul hauled a snapping turtle out of the muck, an old one, about the size of the tire rims that appeared when the lake ebbed, rusty in the mud.

Den had bound the turtle's jaws with fishing line, and they'd rowed back across the lake to the beach with the turtle staring yellow-eyed at them, flapping his flippers helplessly, his plastron flat to the deck. When they got to the beach, Den set the turtle down in the midst of the crazy quilt of beach towels and cut the snapper's jaws free with his penknife. The turtle snapped his way through the squealing girls who scattered before him. As he slapped into the water, the turtle gave a last final snap, punctuating Linda White's ankle with a red caret. Mrs. White phoned my mother.

This time Paul took my mother's prohibition on the Dorman boy seriously. I didn't see them together for a week. Paul moped around the house, listlessly reading Dell monster comics, gluing together airplane models only to push them, single-winged and decal-less, aside. A few times I approached him. "Do you want to go frog hunting?" "Do you want to go shoot BBs at dump rats?" But Paul only shook his head and stared out the picture window at the lake.

———

Rachel splashes water in Toby's face. He closes his eyes. His water-beaded cheeks make him look as if he's crying. But he shakes his head and opens his eyes. "Stop it," he yells at Rachel. She grins her nippy grin and splashes him again. Beyond earshot, her father floats, just below Clarks' pastureland. "I said stop it," Toby hollers again. I appraise Rachel. She's easily got four years and twenty pounds on Toby who's just seven, a June bug like Paul and me. I consider intervening, but I'll wait until Toby's pitch reaches crisis. A mother's intervention can damage a boy. Let him fend for himself, I steel myself. But I feel the neural tingle as I urge my muscles to relax against their will. Rachel's father floats. At this distance he might be a log or light dancing on a wind-whipped whitecap. A flash of green, a flash of belly, a dipping limb.

He's ringed by the far side of the lake. We grew up just calling it the far side as if it were capitalized in our imaginations. Everyone in town knew the far side referred to the lake. Woods gnarled the far side. Hardhack tangled and choked the deer clearings where the herd grazed. No one built summer camps there. Perhaps a duck or deer blind, but nothing more ambitious. Moose reputedly browsed on the far side. Coy dogs sprinted over deadfall trunks. Raccoons chattered. Bucks rutted.

Wild turkeys gabbled and woodcocks protecting their young whirred in feathery flurries at intruders. I don't know why no one built cottages or camps on the far side. Perhaps the lack of access roads. Perhaps the land's state-owned. But the far side remained wild, wilder than the coterminous wilderness. Aside from pastureland, most of Vermont was untamed then. A few villages sprinkled along the rivers. A few farms popped up like dandelions on the hillside. But even for a wooded area like Healdville, the far side was unsettled. When I first learned Paul had built a camp there with Den I didn't believe it.

Rachel has tippytoed out to the point where Toby can't reach her without going over his head. He looks back at me once, his eyes a bafflement of embarrassment and beseeching. But he can't bring himself to ask me for help. Rachel cups a hard splash at him. "Stop it," he screams at her, but his eyes remain fixed on me. Hold your ground, Toby. Not yet. Don't give in yet. I open the front page of the paper over my face, a screen. It rustles in the stiffening wind. I peek once around the edge at Rachel. Eleven, I estimate, about the age I was when I hung out with Linda and her friends. What were their names? Lisa; no, Lizzie. I remember. We sang that song, "You Make Me Dizzy Miss Lizzie." Lizzie was the pretty one, blonde rippled hair, a freckled nose, chocolaty eyes. And the other girl, stout but solid like a fireplug, an ordinary name, Cathy or Debbie? I dig my toes into the sun-warmed sand. The beach chair mesh mashes the backs of my thighs. I'll have to take a swim soon; the sun's hot. Sweat beads and trickles between my breasts. A runny, distracting sensation. Polly, that was it. The other girl's name was Polly.

Linda, Lizzie, Polly, and I were adrift in the *Miss Tipsy* the day the crab apple war broke out. We were floating toward the reeds in one of the far side's shallows. Trout darted beneath the boat's shadow. Our conversation skimmed and jerked along the surface of the day like water bugs on the lake. Lizzie was telling us something about her training bra. "Training for what?" Polly demanded. "Boob camp," Linda blurted. And that launched us into one of those skirling titter-binges we were prone to at that age. It didn't take much.

I was the first to sight the prow of Den's rowboat poking from one of the island channels. The boat was riding low. As it stroked nearer, the figures focused. I could discern Paul on the middle thwart, rowing with

Den. Two of the Howell boys, older even than Den by a year or two, sat on the aft thwart. My second cousin, Tamson, nicknamed Tammie by her parents and Tommie by everyone else in town, was hanging over the bow. Tommie was seventeen, the oldest of the group. She'd been a notorious tomboy until she suddenly became a notorious town girl. She started hanging out with a widowed farmer in Marbleville, and everyone said she was doing it although we weren't sure what. She still dressed boyishly, flapping tennis shoes, baggy suntan shorts and her father's cast-off T's. I assumed they were fishing and I waved. Paul and Den stroked, but Tommie waved back.

They took us entirely by surprise. One minute we were sun-drunk and hazily content. Then a pelting hail of hard crab apples strafed the boat, thunking into the side of the dinghy, plopping onto the floor. "Hey, what the—?" Polly was quick. She scooped apples from the floor and hurled them back at whooping Den who was standing up, straddling the thwart for best aim. Tommie's softball pitching arm was still good. She pumped the hard apples at us. I threw a few, wild and wide. The Howell boys returned another volley. Only Paul sat, just sat and watched, his eyes a dare to me: If you tell Mom, I'll . . . But maybe I imagined that. I didn't have much time to stare. "They must have bushels of them," Polly hollered. Her teeth showed in a smile, grim but pleased, as she tossed a clip that caught Den off balance. Lizzie and Linda crouched, huddling under their hands opened like umbrellas against the hail. "Return fire," I heard Tommie shout. Another salvo. A crab apple whistled into my cheek. Polly leaned over the gunwale to fish out some apples. "Retreat," Tommie shouted. "Pull." And Den and Paul pulled, but unevenly. The rowboat zigzagged behind the cover of the island. "Why those sons of sapsuckers," Polly said, and she scrambled upright to get off one parting shot. My heart lurched with the dinghy as Polly struggled to recover her balance and dumped us all into the lake. We sank to our knees in the muck with Lizzie squealing and eeking about snapping turtles, and Polly issuing orders to right and bail the boat for reboarding, which took several efforts and hours, the mud unyielding, the boat as tippy as her name implied, and the transom a shin-banging couple of inches too high.

I could have tattled on Paul, but I didn't. I told my mother about the crab apples, but I didn't tell her about Den. I populated my story

with the Howell boys and Paul and Tommie and some other kid I didn't
know. "It sounds harmless enough," Mom said, "just a boy-girl thing."

"Then why was Tommie involved?" I demanded.

My mother only shrugged and smiled an infuriating smile, secretive
and knowing.

And I accepted it much as I'd accepted the discovery, as we paddled
back across the lake, that my response to the apple attack differed from
the other girls'. Each seemed to enjoy it. "I got in a few good licks,"
Polly said, blade in the water, huffing happily as she pulled against the
wind. "I'd like to get me a T-shirt like Tommie's," Linda mused. "I think
it's cool." Lizzie dangled her feet over the side of the dinghy, dabbling
her toes in the water. "What do you think of Den Dorman?" she asked
generally. Den Dorman? I'd never thought anything about him. He
was a kid who was born looking like the man he'd become, his chest
muscled, his arms corded. In his father's store, he wore a T-shirt, but
once outdoors he stripped it off and ran through summer, mud-brown
and warm. "I think he's trouble," I said.

"He has a good arm," Polly commented. "A damn good arm."

"Mom hired him last summer to clean the stable," Linda said. She
shrugged. "He never talked to me. Heck, he was a high school kid. But
he seemed okay, okay with the horses."

"Mmm," Lizzie said. She lifted her blonde hair and twisted toward
us. "Well, I think he's cute."

"Cute?" Polly stopped rowing. Linda and Lizzie giggled. "Cute's for
babies," Polly said and resumed rowing.

I sat containing my own response, each apple's insult rising like the
red welt on my cheek. Each of Tommie's hoots humiliated me in a way
I didn't understand. Pummeled by the firm rounds, by their laughter as
we dodged and ducked, I'd felt helpless, more helpless still as I'd peered
across the water at Paul who sat as still as one of his unfinished plane
models. That summer we engaged in other crab apple skirmishes, from
the first encounter on, forearmed with windfall crab apples we carted
from the beach. Den always fired the first shot. Sometimes he chose to;
sometimes he chose not to. Den called the shots. It depended on his
mood or the fishing. But I never saw Paul lob an apple. Not one.

He became strange to me that summer, one of the rangy boys who
listened to transistors at the lake, twisted their soaked towels into rattails

to snap at the girls. When I passed near his towel at the beach, he didn't blink. He didn't see me. I might have registered more hurt, but I had Lizzie, and Linda, and Polly now and our high-pitched helium-giddy fits of giggles and conversation lifted me beyond hurt. And I may have understood that what friendship Paul and I had had as brother and sister depended entirely on me. I could step into his world of rusty bait cans and oily BB guns, but he could never make raspberry jam with Mom and me or sew quilted potholders for the guild fair. We didn't expect him to; it would have violated some implicit law. I could move from domestic interiors to tramp with Paul through the outdoors. But the door between inside and out swung more freely out than in. Paul no longer admitted me, but I could row the lake with girlfriends, curry horses with Linda, hike logging roads with Polly. I was at a loss for neither company nor activity; the days filled themselves.

Rachel's father surfaces alongside the raft. He grabs the ladder and hefts himself up. He rises between the arched handrails, head, shoulders, torso, legs. Fully there, he snaps his waistband. "Hey, honey," he calls to Rachel with a wide metronomic wave of his arm, click, clack. Click, clack. "Hey, Rache. Ra-chel." His daughter pauses, neglecting Toby's torment momentarily to wave back. Pleased, the father drops to his knees, lowers himself onto his stomach to sun-dry on the decks.

I remember the warm burlap that used to carpet the raft, its rough nap scraping my skin, its warm rotted hemp smell. The beach committee used to haul the raft each fall, scrape off the old burlap, tack on the new feed bags before resetting the raft each spring. The burlap was supposed to keep kids from slipping on the wet planks. But some of the boys used to dive to the bottom, return with scoops of mud, and smear the burlap with muck. Then they'd slip and slide, wrestling each other for the title of king of the raft. Den usually reigned. When people swam too near, he'd catapult gobs of mud from his stockpiles at the pretenders. He'd smear himself with the muck, too, let it air-dry, cake and flake off. Then he'd dive into the water, sluicing off the mud, swim to shore to bask with his friends on the boulders by the picnic area. When Den was mud-king, I just swam in the other direction. That's why I'm surprised even now that I could not swim away from my curiosity about the far side camp.

Lizzie, Linda, Polly, and I were lying in the shade beneath the maples on the beach knoll, wearing the look-alike oversized T's we'd lifted from our fathers' drawers and Tommie's sense of style. As Linda chattered on about dressage, I plucked heads of clover, sucking the sweetness from the tiny nodes at the base of the purple petals, catching occasional snatches of the conversation wafting up from the boulders where Paul and Den sprawled. I overheard Den bragging about how they'd built the best fort anyone had ever built in Healdville.

I didn't doubt that they'd built a fort. I didn't doubt that they'd built an elaborate fort. All the boys in town built camps. The Howells had built a two-story tree house with a porch. And Tommie had built a one-room log cabin on Dump Road with a woven pine branch roof. What I doubted was that they'd built the fort on the far side. I started paying more attention to the Dormans' rowboat, and several times noticed it nosing into the far side shore, not far from the shallows where Polly had capsized *Miss Tipsy*. In August, without understanding my own motives, I began keeping my own company. I no longer drifted in *Miss Tipsy* with the girls but chose instead to head down to our shore property, overturn the red canoe and paddle solitary across to the far side. My arms grew strong with paddling. I felt I could cross the lake in a few strong strokes. The far side was nearer than I'd thought.

I oiled the red canvas of the canoe to keep it supple. The varnished wood of the canoe's strutwork gleamed. It had a skeletal spareness that pleased me as I daily paddled the red canoe, parting reeds, slicing into the little inlets along the shore. Eventually, by the broken branches and beaten-down brush, I identified the spot where Den and Paul must land and haul up the boat. It was shadowy there and cool, slipping in and out of the overhanging branches with their sharp pungence, balsam and hemlock. I paddled tentatively, peering through the woods. But I saw nothing unexpected until the day I spotted the rowboat, snugged up against a birch sapling. And with a quickening heart, I realized I'd discovered the vicinity of Paul and Den's camp. I paddled softly back across the lake. But I ached with an unsatisfied longing, a longing to know more about the world Paul and Den had created.

I tossed that night. My nightgown bunched uncomfortably in my armpits, and the sheets coiled serpentine around me. I unwound myself, stripped the top sheet from my bed, yanked my gown over my head, and stood by my open window, letting the lake breeze cool me. Then a second chill prickled my skin. I heard my father's low voice singing or crying. I could not tell which. But I knew that while his days were restful, his nights were restless, sleepless. I listened to the watery rise and fall of his voice, a sorrow emerging and submerging, the song of a drowning man until, unable to bear it any longer, hot as it was, I lowered the window sash as quietly as I could. The counter-weights long ago worn off the pulley ropes, I removed the prop. With a thunk, the sash dropped like a guillotine blade.

I woke clammy and cranky and longing for the cool of the lake. After a breakfast of shredded wheat, I helped my mother with chores, incinerating the trash, picking berries, pinning the laundry. Paul was off pitching hay bales for the Clarks. "Is he working all day?" I asked Mom.

She didn't hear me until I repeated the question. "He's working as long as they want him," she said. Then with her apron hammocky with a heap of unused clothespins, she disappeared into the cellar hatchway. I watched Dad's plaid bathrobe flutter on the line, uncertain for a moment whether I'd be missed. Then I slipped off through the field toward the shore.

I crossed the lake quickly. My dad's T-shirt, damp with perspiration, plastered my back. But once I reached the far side I slowed, my urgency strange to me. The clinging shirt eased. My skin cooled. I turned the canoe slowly, gracefully, the paddle tilted like a rudder. Then I resumed paddling, patient now, enjoying the shuck, shuck of the blade in the water, the green mossy smell of the shore. I recognized the landing spot. I aimed for it. The red curve of canoe penetrated the twiggy bush. A monarch fluttered into the sun. With a jolt, the canoe ran aground. I stepped forward and pulled the canoe up, none of these actions planned, all proceeding from some instinctive curiosity to see the camp.

Toby's screams divert my attention from the newspaper I'm reading blindly. Rachel's hopping on his shoulders now, dunking him. That's intervention time. I make the big T, time-out, sign with my hands as I start from my chair, all knees and elbows, lurching. Toby's blubbering, tears and lake water. A gurgling scream before Rachel plunges him

back under. My voice is out of control, sonar-pitched, and flittery as
bat flight. "Stop it. Stop it. You're drowning him." I plunge my hands
underwater. Ice water. My hands silvery cold as they grope for Toby's
shoulder, fumble for his armpits, lift him catfish-gaping into the air.
"You could have killed him," I scream, my voice flapping away from
me. "You could have killed him." Toby clutched to my chest, I stride
through the water. I hear Rachel's father rousing behind me on the
raft. "I'm sorry. Jesus." The splash as he dives in. The sobs in Toby's
chest are pressed so hard into my chest, they could be rising in me.
Still cradling him, I drop to the sand. The sobs already intersperse with
longer intervals between. He's crying more quietly now. Not fear sobs.
The sad embarrassed weeping of someone who's revealed his fear. I
glance up. Rachel's father is holding her, too, holding her, shaking her,
yelling into her face, "How could you do that? How could you do such
a stupid, stupid thing?" The way he enunciates "stupid," repeating it,
makes Rachel cry. He is telling her a truth, one of those truths that
reveals itself only through action, one of those truths that slips out
under words. Fish, shadows of fish, darting under lily pads.

━━━━━━━━

A truth of happening. This is what happened. After I pulled the
canoe up, I looked for snapped twigs. I found a spot on a tree trunk
where a deer or moose had rubbed the velvet from its antlers. I found
a fallen robin's nest on the roots of an ash. A squirrel chattered at me
from the crotch of the tree as it cracked a seed in its teeth. I detected
a path, a slightly trampled passage through the brush, and I followed.
As I entered deeper into the woods, I saw stumps where trees had been
deliberately felled, piles of sawdust, the trunks stubbed, raw and conical,
as yellow-white as worn canines.

I walked through the forest silence with a similar silence, an unquiet
quiet, the quiet staccato of snapped twigs, held breaths, blinking eyes.
A quiet of suspended sound. A sentient silence full of hollows and
deliberateness. The near-silence of a sigh.

The woods smelled decadent and mulchy. Shadows shivered in the
quivery filters of green light sifting through the leaves. Wind snarled
high in the branches somewhere above where the sky still maintained
itself. A limb snapped beneath my sneaker. I jumped as if the branch

had determined to snap. I stared at ruffles of gray lichen on a tree trunk. What was conscious, what was accidental, became confused. My stomach said it was hungry. But I couldn't track the sun. Was it lunchtime? The trees tented me in shadow. I heard small scurries. Chipmunks? Time sank. Healdville fell away. Paul trying to float. My feet found their own way. My hand smudged as I vaulted over a rotted trunk. Rocks, huge outcrops of rocks shouldering their way up. Humus. And then I saw it. The camp.

It sprawled, following an architectural logic of its own. The center was an enclosed circle of spiked, vertical logs hung with moose racks. Circumscribed, another circle of stones enclosed the remains of a campfire. A ramp rose from the center, careened crazily back on itself before doubling back again, leading to a platform from which a ladder ascended to an enclosed room built with four trees as corner posts. A tatter of plain bed sheet fluttered from a pole. Beside it an iron wheel rim dangled, the spokes twisted with vines. Paper bull's-eye targets dotted with BB shot fluttered on a rail fence. The stove-in hull of a boat, bow up, arched like a sentry box from a corridor leading out of the circle across from the ramp. The corridor led to another ladder, crosspieces nailed into a pine tree, which rose to another ramp and tree house, from which a rope ladder dangled. Beyond the circle, two tepee structures of lashed saplings and pine bows rose like spires. The structure was crude but intricate. Ambitions aspiring beyond their raw materials: junk, logs, brush, rotted wood, rope, a few nails. Beside the campfire, a sign tilted from the ground. I approached to read it. Roughly carved, it read simply, "Camp." I turned, thought briefly about climbing the ramp or ladder, but knew whatever curiosity had urged me here was satisfied. I headed for the aperture in the ring.

I don't know how long they'd been watching me. I know only this: a rush of sound, like blood in your ears. A thunk from behind, my hands braceleted behind me, I fell airlessly onto my chest with a weight on my back, a voice. "Well, Paul. What do you think she's doing way over here?"

While Den jerked me back to my feet, while Den kept up his patter, "I think she should pay a forfeit for violating the sanctuary, don't you, Paul?" while Den banged me face first into a tree at the rim of the circle,

I could not see him. I could see only his voice pulsing in the air and Paul's eyes, which disclosed nothing. Den spun me around.

"What price do you think little girls should pay for trespassing in a boys' camp?" he asked.

I stared at Paul, who stood still as a jacked buck, frozen in a headlight beam. "Paul," I called his name, but I couldn't hear it.

Den twisted his fist in the hem of my T-shirt. A pitchy smear of pine needles and dirt slashed diagonally across the shirt. He pushed his face into mine, so near I could feel the warmth of his breath in the air I inhaled. "Maybe we should see her titties, Paul?" His eyes did not leave my face. "Eh, Paul?"

My nipples hardened. Crab apples. Red. I stared past Den into Paul's blank eyes. A horror between my legs. My mother's cleaver halved a raw potato that split into a brown core squirming with earwigs. Teeming. They squiggled over the grain bands of the damage board, spilled onto the kitchen counter as my mother squealed. The knife clattered to the floor. "Show us your titties," Den said. His fingers tugged at the hem of my father's shirt. Peripherally, his left hand, his right. Something moving. "No," I said, looking at Paul. The hands moving toward the white of my father's shirt. And then it's oozing, wet. Chokecherries smashing red into white cotton. Den's grinding hands, grinding laugh. A red stain above red heart. A pulse. I knew I'd bitten him because my mouth ran chokecherry red and tasted ferrous and salty like blood. But fear tasted like that, too. I knew I was crying because the red stain grew blurry, became me. I knew I was running because trees were crashing by me. Bark snagged my hair. Twigs whipped smartly against my cheeks. A tree trunk banged into my hip. A root humped up to trip me. I broke surprised from the bank, broke like an egg into yolky sun, sank knee-deep into mud, stumbled back to find the canoe, hearing laughter far away like bird cries. Like cries. Two cries. Den and Paul's. Two eyes. Too still eyes.

When I gained our shore property, I beached the canoe and swam fully clothed trying to bleach out, rinse the dirt and berry red from my shirt. When I banged into the kitchen, my mother asked, "What happened to you?"

"I tipped over in the canoe," I said.

"For goodness sake, get out of those wet things," Mom said. "Go change."

I did. I bathed and changed into one of my nicest dresses, a rose gingham dress that had become too worn for church. Pink from the bath, my skin felt happy against the matching, soft cloth.

My dad shambled out to join us for dinner, his bathrobe cinched.

"You look pretty, princess," he said, bussing my cheek.

"Thank you."

Paul ate, eyes lowered to his plate.

Like water, night closed over the house, fall over summer, silence over the day that dropped between us like a pebble. Dark ripples from one hard action. A tossed stone. Crab apple. Dropped sinker. BBs shot in a mud puddle. Concentric rings. At center, we were not the same.

My father's sickness moved into the red house that summer, its tenancy grandfathered in. It remained until his death. He fought the cancer for a surprising five years. The summer of his death my mother painted the house white as if she were snapping a bed sheet clean or a summer blanket, spring-cleaning disease from the house.

Rachel's father rocks beside me on the beach, cradling his snuffling girl much as I'm cradling Toby. "We must be quite a pair of bookends," he says in a tone that means to apologize.

I shake my head and hem noncommittally. I don't want to involve myself in conversation. I don't want to involve myself. But he's a stream of words babbling over a bed of polished pebbles.

"She hasn't been herself since the divorce. She misses her mother. Her mother actually grew up here, summered over there." He points.

In spite of myself, I look up, following his index finger. Garrisons? I pat Toby's back. Garrisons?

"Rachel's mine. But I'm not the first husband. I'm the second. And Tammie's already got a third."

Tommie? Tommie?

"It's hard on Rachel. The new husband. They don't get along. When we were married, Tam and I, we used to rent that last cabin there, at the edge of the pasture?" He rolls Rachel toward his stomach, freeing up his arm just enough to point in the opposite direction.

"How is Tammie?" I ask, hating myself. I'm just getting in deeper, but I want to know.

"Tammie? You know Tam. Well, she's great. I mean she's the same. Oh, she worked as a carpenter for a while. Now she's waiting table at The Quiet Woman in Castleton." Rachel shifts her weight in her father's lap. She presses her cheek against his chest and turns her face toward Toby.

Toby shifts, too. I crane my neck to see his face. His eyes return her stare. He's quiet, his mouth plugged with a finger.

In the children's silence, I hear the voice of the lake, the voice of the lake in summer, always one echoing voice, Rachel's, Toby's, Paul's, Tommie's, mine. Always the same chord of shrieks playing off the mountains toothing the mouth of the lake. A fading evening sound of mosquitos, frogs, dragonflies, the last boat chuttering home.

The father gently shunts Rachel aside and wipes his palm on his bathing trunks. "Keith," he introduces himself. "Keith Towson."

I hesitate. What does the exchange of names imply? Will I have to talk to him now when I see him at the beach? Will I have to simper while his daughter drowns my son? I take his hand and shake it, feeling the weight of Toby's stillness in my lap, hearing his stare whistle through the air to Rachel who gazes back. I peer into her eyes, hoping for remorse, but find there only the murky green of lake water. Why, oh why? I ask myself. Something loosing from me, slipping, a red ellipse across a green stillness. A truth that comes from understanding nothing. A splash. A plunk.

"Sandy. Sandy Hall." I release his hand. I drop my name.

THE ATTIC

"WE'RE ALL SO DAMN COMPLEX," Dad announces to his fifth glass of wine.

Patrick flinches, mutters, "maudlin," aside to Janice, his wife, who lowers her eyes to her lap, embarrassed.

"More turkey anyone?" Mom asks. My mother has a remarkable sense of what the family long ago nicknamed "The Statement Incongruous."

"Complex," my father insists again, glaring at my mother.

"Well, it's more than we can say for the wine," I answer pouring another goblet of Hearty Burgundy.

Appreciatively, my father smiles. "Only my daughter has inherited my fine sensibility," he says clinking his glass against mine.

"Yes," Patrick agrees, the familiar, hard glint in his eye, "the fine balance between maudlin drunkenness and that irrepressible Irish wit."

"Well then, a piece of pie perhaps," mother offers, "a nice cup of coffee?"

My father slouches and eyes his wine glass glumly, silencing his tongue.

I think, every Thanksgiving, a bit of the family tradition to rehearse the old bitterness, to repeat the unforgivable phrase, to stretch the ties of family loyalty to their snapping point only to relax them and regret them in the morning.

"An ungrateful son-of-a-bitch. Always was," Dad mumbles. "You will never know just what I've given up, just how damn good a man I am. Damn good," he adds emphatically, and rubs the faded scar above his brow.

Janice is my mother's daughter under her skin, born with an instinct to ignore unpleasantness. "I'll get the pie," Janice says too cheerily, clearing the dishes. She and my mother bustle, clattering dishes into the sink. Dad stares at the congealed grease on his plate.

Impatiently, Patrick gets up and joins my mother. They whisper together. "I can't take another year like this," he hisses. "For God's sake put away the bottle." And my mother's answering whisper, "Just humor him. He's tired, dear."

"The Greeks," my father roars. Mom drops the gravy ladle. Patrick moans. He descends the three steps into the living room, hides behind a copy of the *Smithsonian* in an easy chair. I perk up. This is my favorite part.

"The Greeks. Law and order. Civilization. Order and beauty. Now they had a sense of proportion."

I nod encouragingly at my father.

"The ideal limb. The perfect nose. Architecture," my father booms.

Patrick can't contain himself. "And sticking it to a philosopher up the bunghole," he yells from the living room.

"Your brother's very ordinary, you know," my father says, spreading his large hand over mine. "No imagination. Rather a crude specimen, really."

My mother flutters around the table, smoothing out napkins, salting wine stains. The pie appears. I think, For years my mother has offered dessert as a sweetness to ease this bitterness. Sugar to confound anger. Honey to cloy and dull the palate.

"Sugar for your coffee, dear?" Mom asks my father hopefully.

"No coffee," he grunts, "it gets on my nerves." The same response year after year.

"Patrick," Janice calls, "dessert," knowing Patrick's sweet tooth aches, gets the better of his pique. He grumbles back to the table and sits down. Thanksgiving, I think, a family confection. I note my father's wedge of pie, untouched, unmarred by fork tines—the ideal pie, perfection of proportion, cuneiform.

"The Greeks," my father lectures, using his fork as a pointer, "were a noble race. A race of poet-philosophers finely tuned to the music of the spheres. Poetry, a touch of madness, and reason, the good sense to temper it."

Patrick struggles, wanting to throw down his fork in disgust, a symbolic gesture. But there sits the pie, rich, brown, half-eaten. He takes another bite, content to appear sullen.

Dad pours another glass of wine. My mother, always alert to *discordia humana*, asks Patrick, "How are things in the office?" Patrick is a lawyer. He briefs her on his cases, one eye cocked warily on Dad, one on his pie, while my mother "um's" and "ah's" and "isn't that nice's."

"Siobhan," my father turns to me; he reverts to my Gaelic name half-way through a bottle.

"Yes," I ask.

"Siobhan. That's your name in Gaelic," he says, shaking his head as if names were a weighty matter.

Distracted, Patrick appeals to my mother, "Not the Irish theme. The Greek is easier to take than the Irish."

"Siobhan," my father says again, slightly louder, and recites, " 'The Irish are the race that God made mad. Their wars are all happy; their loves are all sad.' "

"Dear, you haven't touched your pie," my mother interrupts. Sugar for your wine, I think. "Won't you try your pie?" Mom asks, coaxing.

"My family does not understand me," my father tells me. I nod. I think, it is fortunate that my family has the knack to go deaf at will. Deaf, of course, but never dumb.

Patrick throws down his fork, his pie and his gesture at last completed. "I'm fed up!" This—my father chooses to hear.

"You're fed up. You're fed up?" he asks. Familiar crescendo. "Jesus, Mary, and Joseph, I'm up to here with family." He draws his fork across his throat. "Once a year you come to eat my food and throw it in my face. Interrupt my work. Bite the hand that's fed you all these years. Marion," he addresses my mother, "I'm going to the attic and do some work. Enough of this." He flings himself indignantly from the table and clumps heavily up the stairs, slams the door, sealing himself off in the attic.

Janice's eyes wax full as harvest moons; she's not used to all this yet. "He'll be all right in the morning," Mom says. Patrick peels a tangerine.

In the living room, Patrick tries to enlist support while I stoke the fire in the stove. " 'Work,' " Patrick says incredulously, "he's too drunk to work. The man's impossible."

"Retirement's been hard on him," Mom says complacently above the clack, clack, clack of her knitting needles.

Janice watches Patrick, a good wife trying to share her husband's hurt. Patrick joins her on the couch, grimaces at my mother, "You're always defending him."

"Clack, clack, clack," her knitting needles answer him.

"He's a complicated man," I say. "You should try to understand him." I shove a birch log into the stove and watch the papery bark curl off in flames.

"Understand him. My God. You're just like him," Patrick accuses me. "You're the golden girl, the sun, the moon, Artemis, Apollo's darling. Everything for the golden girl," Patrick sneers. "But what has he done for me?"

So familiar, the family script. I shrug at Patrick—he's a masterful sneerer—and grin, knowing my nonchalance irritates the hell out of him.

"A series of clichés. The man's a series of clichés." Patrick presents his case. "For years it was, 'We're all so damn unique,' then 'Art is the only justification for life,' or, alternately, 'Life justifies itself.' Now it's, 'We're all so damn complex.' "

"It's just a part of aging, dear," my mother says, her voice gentle. "You'll understand when you get older."

"I've been hearing that all my life," Patrick spouts.

"Don't shout," Mom warns. "You'll disturb your father. When you have children, you'll do the same thing." The Statement Incongruous.

"He doesn't know squat," Patrick persists, "about the Greeks, about law, even about the goddamned Irish. The man's a fraud."

"Well he tries, dear." My mother knits. Janice sits. I close the door to the stove, sneak up to the dining room, and rescue the wine bottle from the table before Mom tucks it away. I crook my finger in the handle and sling the jug over my shoulder, peace offering, and tiptoe up the stairs. A tread creaks.

"Brownnoser," Patrick yells.

I love my father.

I knock on the door to the attic. No answer. Deliberate deafness. The attic is not really an attic but my father's study, his retreat. My father has drawn huge circles of isolation around this room. Concentric circles—

Vermont, a small town, acres of forests and hills, the last house on a dirt road, this farmhouse—all circumscribe this focal point, the attic, where he huddles in his solitude. Withdrawing inward, ever inward upon himself, although I remember a time, before his operation, when we lived in town, my father, the gregarious host, the house noisy with people and my father's jokes. "It's all a part of aging," my mother says.

It's cold in the hall. I knock on the door again. "It's me, Dad," I say. He cracks the door. "It's *I*," he corrects. "The verb 'to be' always takes the nominative." And I step into his room. The walls are fortified with rows of books. On the shelves, small replicas of pillars, Doric simplicity, Ionic stateliness, Corinthian ostentation. The ruins from his years of teaching art history, architecture. On the floor, reams of paper, clipped articles, an orderly chaos. He knows where everything is as if it were filed neatly away. On the wall, a Celtic cross, a map of Ireland, Scottish bagpipes, "an udderly barbaric sound," Dad's ancient pun.

"You've brought the jug," he smiles, satisfied, and slumps into his desk chair. "I just can't help myself," he apologizes. "Family's too many for me."

I pass him the jug and sit in his rocking chair.

"You can't control people. Too large a margin for error," he says and takes a slug from the bottle. "History I can understand. All history, that is, except family history: a perpetual work in progress, a confusing compendium of footnotes." He nods in appreciation of his metaphor, then sighs. "I don't understand Patrick. I never have."

"We all have our blind spots," I say, exchanging cliché for cliché, thinking Patrick is right: a series of clichés.

"We change, but we don't change," Dad says staring out of the window at nothing, indistinguishable mountains that he knows are there only by habit, the black night. I see his face mirrored in the glass darkly, white beard, laugh creases, tired eyes in the reflected halo of lamp light.

" 'For now we see through a glass darkly,' " Dad recites, " 'but then face to face: now I know in part; but then shall I know even as also I am known.' "

For a moment I am startled by the reflection of my own thought, then dismiss the coincidence. Dad's favorite verse; he has recited it often.

"One Corinthians, thirteen: twelve," he cites. He tips the jug again and continues, "In here, I know who I am. Order. The printed word . . ."

He trails off sleepily. "Why does he keep coming home if I make him so miserable?" he asks, suddenly rousing. "Where does it all end?" He picks up his own train of thought, "I think we've rehearsed my guilt thoroughly enough. Act one, scene one: I didn't let Patrick name his own dog. Frisky. 'Frisky,' for that noble hound. Zeus! And Patrick called him 'Zeussie.'" Dad shakes his head. "Act two, I forced him to wear brush cuts when barbarian hair lengths were the fashion." He enumerates the episodes on his fingers. "And my tragic flaw, of course, my unforgivable sense of timing, contracting cancer when Patrick was only fourteen. Unthinkable." Dad pours wine absent-mindedly into his dirty coffee cup, swings the jug toward me. "Cancer, I was born under Cancer, born under a bad sign."

Uncomfortable, I shift, not because the revelations are new, but because, since Dad's cancer went into remission nine years ago, the family tries not to discuss it, as if it were an embarrassment, a failure of the will—like alcoholism.

"June twenty-second. The crab," Dad continues, "ruled by the moon. Sometimes I think your brother would have preferred this crab to scuttle off the mortal coil."

I shake my head, but my father chooses not to see it.

"I will never forget when I came home, swathed in bandages like some mummy. Patrick swore at me. My own son swore at me."

My father slaps his hand down on the desk. "Through years of treatments, he moped around the house, sullen—pouting at me as if I'd done it on purpose. What did he want from me?" He grips the arms of his chair so tightly, I wonder if wood can bruise. But I don't answer. We've considered all the answers before: a healthy father, reassurance Dad would live, love, attention? Who knows? I don't think Patrick knows. Sometimes we all grow weary of the questions posed by the past. It's relentless, bootless like some querulous history teacher trying to scold answers out of the class with a ruler.

"Just what does he want?" my father asks, readjusting the tense of the question.

I wonder if the question is theatrical, but venture an answer anyway, "Maybe he wants you to forget."

"I'll forget when he does."

I wonder if forgetting is willful or accidental. We sit quietly together.

I watch his head droop forward on his chest, jerk occasionally against sleep. For a while, I listen to him snore; then I stash the jug under his desk before creeping off to tell Mom he's fallen asleep.

Downstairs Patrick lies full-length on the couch, so my mother and Janice sit on the floor looking into the opened door of the wood stove. I sit cross-legged next to my mother.

"Did you have a nice visit, dear?" Mom asks looking up from her knitting.

"Dad's asleep," I answer.

Patrick grumbles to no one in particular, "When are you finally going to get a TV?"

I dart a wicked look at my mother. "That *reductio ad absurdum* of existence? That barbarism of banality?" I'm a careful understudy.

Patrick snaps to a sitting position. "You're drunk. You're always drunk," he yells. "Isn't she drunk?" he appeals to my mother.

Janice scoots her butt nearer my mother. Mom pats her knee as she says, "Well, doesn't everyone think it's time for bed?"

Janice leaps at the chance and the stairs, but, as she passes Patrick, the good wife relents. "Won't you come to bed, honey?" she asks.

"I will not be placated," Patrick booms like some thunder god.

I roll my eyes. "Don't wake your father," my mother says as she creaks up the stairs, Janice only one creak behind her.

I hear my father, above-stairs, grumbling as my mother wakes him, hear the sleepy shuffle, the murmur behind closed doors. I glance at Patrick, familiar scowl. Silently I check the arsenal, sharpen my Statement Incongruous, hone my Irish wit, my Greek rationality: the family jewels.

Patrick plants his feet on the floor, sets his square Irish jaw, pinches his eyes. "Why do you have to suck up to him, for God's sake?"

I hear water splashing, Janice washing her face, brushing her teeth. The Statement Incongruous: "Would you like a cup of tea?" I ask Patrick, holding my hands, palms out, toward the stove.

"Tea," Patrick echoes.

"Hush," I say. "You'll wake Dad." It helps to know the script.

Patrick punches a cushion on the couch. "This freaking family. Everyone's always tiptoeing around him. The man's a despot."

I pretend to consider this a moment. "You've lost your sense of proportion, Pat."

" 'Proportion.' " His voice is incredulous. I know without looking that his lips are pursed. I anticipate his lines; they come right on cue.

"Christ you even talk like him." Patrick's feet splay out on the floor in front of me. His big toe pokes through a hole in his sock. He juts his hip out. " 'You've lost your sense of proportion, Pat,' " he mimics in falsetto. I think, Not a bad impersonation.

"Well you have," I say.

"Have not," he says.

"Have too," I say.

"Have not."

Strophe. Antistrophe. Patrick pads back to the couch, slumps into it.

"Okay, Pat," I say in my best have-it-your-way voice. Then I add, "You won't admit it, but you have lost your sense of proportion." Get out of that one, I think.

"Have not," Patrick rejoins. Feeble feint.

This is getting silly, I think. I'm losing my sense of proportion. I poke the log in the stove, think of my father upstairs. The despot snug in his bed, snoring. A hand moving inadvertently to brush away the dreams like cobwebs from his face. Patrick is quiet. Pitch sizzles and pops as it runs out of the log. Green wood.

A crazy wail suddenly garbles the silence of the room. I'm on my feet. Patrick's hands freeze around mine. "Jesus, Mary, and Joseph," he says, "what the hell's that?" The trembling in my hands spreads, shakes me with laughter. "Turkeys," I splutter, "wild turkeys."

Patrick laughs too, uneasily at first, as he releases my hands. Patrick and I have not touched each other in years. " 'Jesus, Mary, and Joseph,' " I mimic Patrick. Dad's favorite curse.

Patrick makes a brushing movement at his cheek as if he were trying to flick off his fear, his embarrassment. "Jesus, Mary, and Joseph, indeed," he says. "I thought it was the Banshees, thought they'd come for me at last."

I laugh appreciatively. Patrick slouches on the couch again. The gobble trails away, lost somewhere above the house in the pines.

"Do you want a turkey sandwich?" I ask Patrick.

"Sure," he says, surprises me with a turkey gobble and a laugh.

"Bird calls?" I ask. "What's next? The poodle act or the Flying Fodopolos Brothers?"

When I come back with the sandwiches, Patrick is crouching before the stove, stripping curls of birch paper off a log. I hand him a sandwich on a paper plate.

"Do you know what I was just thinking about?" I ask.

Patrick shakes his head, his cheeks bulging with bread.

"Do you remember the story of Leanan-Sidhe Dad used to tell us when we were kids?"

Patrick shakes his head.

"The one about Leanan where she appears to Cahill naked, night after night, by the rock, and he falls in love with her."

Recognition flickers in Patrick's eyes, catches fire. "That's right," he says. "And when he tries to chase her, embrace her, she runs away."

"Until at last," I say, "he writes her love poems, sonnet after sonnet, and she finally lets him into her arms." I try to hollow out my voice, emulate the wind as my father used to. "She lets him into her arms, kisses his neck, and then sucks him blood dry." I do not end the story as Dad used to: Inspire. Expire, followed by a slow exhalation.

Patrick stares at the fire in the stove. "That story used to terrify me," he says.

We are straying from the script, extemporizing, I think, with surprise. For a moment, we listen to the popping of the wood in the stove. For some reason, I think of the attic—not my father's attic, but the one tucked up under the eaves crammed with baby carriages and broken chairs, boxes of pediatrician's bills, children's hands printed with finger paint on paper plates, yellowing photographs of World War II, and reproductions of the Parthenon, the thumb-smudged books Dad used to read to us before the operation. I think, if this were a play, this would be the moment, the *coup de théâtre*, when Patrick opens up the past, causality is clarified; I am this, because my parents were that. Tidy formula.

Patrick interrupts my reverie by jabbing the poker into the stove, raking the embers. He stuffs the paper plate through the door. The firelight plays over new wrinkles in his face. His legs look massive, heavy, like columns of a ruin.

"I'd almost forgotten that story," Patrick says. "I guess some people just love better from a distance. It's safer."

I wonder if he is talking about himself or Cahill. "Memory can play queer tricks," I say, knowing my response is inadequate. I try to remember the six years Dad battled with the cancer. The doctors never seemed to get it all—in and out of the hospital for radiation, chemotherapy. I'm younger than Patrick. When Dad first entered the hospital, I was only ten. They farmed us out separately to relatives, Patrick at Aunt Fay's. They left me with Grandma. I don't think I really understood what cancer was until, years later, Dr. Cross pronounced it in remission. Even then, I didn't give it much thought. At ten, I was too young, at sixteen, too self-absorbed. I try to imagine Patrick understanding, living through the fear. What did it mean to Patrick at fourteen? That he could not bring friends home? The house was always quiet then as if it, too, were waiting for a final prognosis. Did it merely mean no more games of pitch and catch? Did he think he would have to take care of my mother and me? Male responsibility derived from some virtuous movie on the late, late show: "You have to wear the pants in the family now, Son." Or maybe the realization always before him, like Dad hanging around the house in baggy clothes, that he, too, was going to die. I realize I've never asked Patrick what it meant, how he felt in those six years. I've drawn my own conclusions. I remember Dad once described the cancer as "the cells in mutiny against the captain." My mother told him to hush, everything would be fine. And still there was the cancer, a presence in the house, a stranger. I think of the cancer, invading secretly, quietly, nibbling away at healthy tissue.

"Patrick," I ask softly, afraid of my own temerity, "do you remember when Dad, you know, first came home from the hospital?" When Patrick does not answer, I try again, "What did you think when he first came home, Pat?"

Patrick laughs, I do not know why, then says, "You know I thought it was contagious. I thought, then, I'd given it to him, and, other times, I'd think he'd given it to me. Some nights, I wouldn't fall asleep. I thought I could feel the cells inside me . . ."

This is new material. I consider it and cannot find a ready response or question, so I listen as Patrick jostles the poker into the fireplace stand. He averts his face from me, and it occurs to me he is embarrassed.

For some reason, I am too. "I'm tired," he says. "Another swell family get-together."

I don't try to call him back as he crosses the room, clumps up the stairs. He pauses on the landing. "Good night," he whispers. The door closes. I hear rustlings, murmurs. Janice must have woken up, I think.

I stare through the screen. Just embers now. Mentally, I take the family script, crease it carefully and poke it onto the bed of embers, watch it curl into a sheet of ash. Sometimes you've got to put your cares to bed, my mother used to say when she tucked us in. I close the door of the stove. We'll build another fire in the morning.

Good Neighbors ▮▮▮▮

"THAT MAN AND HIS ROSEBUSHES are going to make me dotty."
The screen door punctuates my announcement with a slap.

Cole looks up from his *Chapman's*, his eyebrows arched. "Oh?" he
asks.

"If he could get away with it, he'd blame the dog for the lack of rain."
I glance at the open page. Cole is reviewing knots, sheepshanks, cat's
paws.

Cole smiles. "Houghton and his people have lived in that house for
over a hundred years. They're island. And islanders don't like change."

"Well," I say and cock my arms, prop my fists on my hips, "Coolidge
didn't bring Japanese Beetles to Maine, and beetles are mucking up his
roses—not Coolidge."

Cole glances out the picture window. He isn't really listening to
me. He's checking the lie of the moored boats in the bay for the
wind direction, the water surface for white caps. "I think I'll take the
Afterthought out for a sail to Halfway Rock," he says. "Want to come?"

I smile and shake my head. Cole knows I won't join him. I don't have
sea legs yet. In salt water, I'm still a tadpole. I watch Cole collect his
gear in the Bean bags: cotter pins, safety flares, fenders, foul-weather
gear—marine arcana. Coolidge and I are Vermonters. Our land rises
solid and rocky into air as sharp and cold as ice crystals. We aren't
acclimated to tides and fog and afternoon winds, the geography of
sandbars, salt marshes, rock ledges. We wander around the island
aimlessly like a sailor who cannot read a chart. Maritime illiterates,
two landlubbers, local-color-blind. We have many codes to crack. One
code I've mastered, however: the code of the outsider. Our neighbor,

Houghton, treats me like a tourist. "Off-island," I imagine him tagging me. At home, my people have been thinking, "Flatlander, out-a-stater," for six generations. I don't like being cast by Houghton as some brash transient carrying an ugly culture with me like Naugahyde luggage, unbiodegradable—with scraps littering my trail when I move on. At home, I'm authentic.

I wave goodbye to Cole as he disappears behind the scarp at the shore. He reappears on the rocks at Aaron's Wharf. I watch him haul the John Dory in and row out to the *Afterthought.*

"I've got things to do," I say to Coolidge and scratch her muzzle. Coolidge regards me warily with her brown collie eyes. She's part collie and all mutt. I brought her to the marriage. Love me, love my dog. "Come on, girl," I say. Once out the door, Coolidge streaks for the mudflats to chase the gulls she will never catch. Desire on the wing.

I carry my toolbox to the weather side of the cottage. I slide my knife under the cracked putty and work the knife back and forth against the window pane. The putty crumbles away into dust. It's cool in the shade of the branches. The air smells piney and salty. "I wouldn't do it that way if I were you," a voice booms at my shoulder. I jump, strike a pine branch with my shoulder, poke my chin with the putty knife.

"Crack the glass," Houghton says.

I turn and look at Houghton. His glasses glint beneath the brim of his straw hat. He thrusts his hands into the pockets of his green Dickies workpants. "Come on," he says. "I want to show you something." I follow him to the flower bed that runs along the western length of his shed. "What do you think?" he asks.

"Very nice," I say, stooping, putty knife in hand, pretending to admire the zinnias rising like a blockade around the shed.

"Nice?" he asks.

I recognize Houghton's style. He sidles up to a subject, approaches it obliquely as an upwind hunter in Vermont approaches his buck in the woods. "Nice," I say.

"Well they used to be nice," Houghton says, "before your dog got to them. Now they're all messed up." He plucks a flower blossom and jabs it with his finger. "Look at the petals," he says. "They're falling right out because your dog's been diddling where she doesn't belong." He spikes a petal off with his thumbnail.

"Looks like earwigs to me," I say.

Houghton tilts his hat back on his head. His blue eyes gleam, very bright, young. "What do you know about earwigs?" he asks.

"Well sir," I say as Coolidge trots up, all muddied, "I know they haven't been chasing gulls down in the flats all morning."

Houghton surprises me by leaning over and patting Coolidge. "She's a good dog," he says. "I just don't want her scrabbling in my garden."

"I can tie her up," I offer.

"Heck no," Houghton blurts.

Yesterday Cole and I tethered Coolidge to the ash tree when we went jigging for mackerel. We could hear her howls all the way over to the Stone Pier. She was still yelping when we got home. Six hours. She's nervous; she doesn't know this is home.

"No," Houghton says more calmly. "I'd hate for you to have to tie her up. Couldn't you leave her inside?" he asks.

I shake my head. "She rips out all the window screens."

Houghton rubs his nose. "Did you ever consider keelhauling that dog?" he asks as he turns back to his garden.

"What's keelhauling?" I ask Cole as I wash the supper dishes.

"What?" Cole asks without looking up. He's plotting a course for an overnight cruise. His charts spread over the kitchen table.

"Houghton said we should keelhaul Coolidge, something to do with keeping the dog out of his garden."

Cole laughs. "He was just having you on."

"Oh," I say. I glance out the window over the sink. "Houghton sure keeps his place up," I say.

Cole snaps his parallel rules together. "He does more around the house than he used to," he says. "He used to sail every day before his heart trouble. He had to sell his boat." He shuffles his charts into a pile.

Houghton's house, a Victorian, painted tricolor to highlight the gingerbread, overlooks a trim lawn flanked by granite blocks warning cars where the edge of the right-of-way ends. The zinnias stand like sentinels on either side of the back door.

I rinse a dinner plate. When I look up again, Houghton is sitting on the back steps, Coolidge at his feet, feeding her something—table scraps?—from a yellowware bowl.

I wait until I see the *Afterthought* leave the mooring. I stuff a garbage bag into my pocket. Then I sneak upstairs as if Cole were still in the house. I open the drawers of the bureau in the second bedroom. Alison's clothes are still neatly folded in the drawers. She was Cole's first wife. Cole didn't throw her clothes away after the divorce. "You never know what's going to come in handy on an island," he explained. But the explanation did not dispel the spookiness of Alison's clothes in the drawer, as if she might materialize some morning, rifling through the drawers, trying to decide what to wear. I pull out a shirt, an out-of-style Indian print halter, time-faded. I try it on; it fits me like one of my own old shirts. But a pair of jeans are too tight. I imagine her—about my height and size, slimmer in the hips, her feet, a size larger than mine. Her Dr. Scholls jut out an inch beyond my big toe. I find a cotton T-shirt and pull it on—green leaves and peach blossoms. I decide to wear it. I heap the rest of the clothes into the garbage bag to sneak off to the dump.

The first week in the cottage, I painted the master bedroom and hung new curtains. Alison and Cole bought the cottage together just down the road from Cole's family place, so they could keep the family ties but loosen the knots. Cole rarely talks about Alison. Five years have elapsed since their divorce. He says he doesn't remember much about her. Cole and I were married in the winter. This is my first summer here. For five years mice have been nesting in Alison's clothes, and Cole has not disturbed them. After our wedding, I pawed through Cole's dresser in our home in Pennsylvania. I could not even find a picture of her. But I know from Cole's friends, she was very beautiful. And blonde. I study myself in the mirror over the dresser and run my hand over my dark hair. The silver is flaking off the mirror back. Black gaps jag my reflection. I think divorce is ghostlier than death. Somewhere, someone, who has listened to the intimate rise and fall of your sleeping breath, walks the earth. Alison left Cole in the winter. She moved to New York—a career move—leaving her clothes in the drawer, her leather suitcase, empty, in the closet. She never came back for them.

———————

As I press my fingers against the rope of putty, I feel, for the first time, the privilege of ownership. My fingerprints mark this putty. I seal out the wind and rain. My home. I hear a rustle behind me. Houghton peers over my shoulder. A trowel dangles from his hand.

"Shed water better if you bevel with your knife," he says.

I smooth the putty with my index finger and consider saying, "I've been puttying windows since before you were born," but that would be ridiculous. Houghton's eighty years old this July, so I don't say anything.

"Got a problem in the garden," Houghton says.

"Oh," I say and press the putty against the pane.

"Yup," Houghton says and turns around. I sigh, place the coil of putty on the sill and follow him across the right-of-way.

Houghton pants shallowly as he points to the flower bed. It's a hot day. "Heart," he says and pops a pill into his mouth. "Nitroglycerine."

"Oh," I say, and, not knowing what else to say, I crouch over his marigolds. Three of the golden blossoms lie withering on the fine, rich soil, snipped off at the base of their stalks. "Looks like slugs," I say. When Houghton doesn't respond, I add, "I'm surprised; I didn't think slugs would go near the stink of a marigold."

"Slugs?" Houghton asks.

"Slugs," I say. "Put some ash around the beds. Slugs won't crawl through ashes."

Houghton scratches his nose. "Ash? We don't do that here. A saucer of beer's the thing for slugs. They crawl right in and drown."

"Well," I say walking away, "I wouldn't want slugs whooping it up outside my bedroom window, keeping me up until all hours." I saunter across the right-of-way, singing "Sweet Adelaide" slightly off-key.

"Maybe," Houghton yells after me, "but ashes won't keep your dog the tunket out of my garden."

I sit on the stone wall eating my cucumber sandwich. The stone wall, which runs the length of the backyard, reminds me of home where stone walls crisscross my parents' acreage, demarcating the fields of long-forgotten farmers. In Vermont, people live further apart than they do on the island, so far apart they do not need fences. In the woods separating houses, the neglected stone walls topple over, the boulders fall randomly back into the fields from which the farmers first cleared them, as if nature wanted to remind us we are all only squatters. The only real landowner is the land. I run my hand over the lichened, bumpy surface of the rock. I feel conciliatory after lunch. As I walk back to the cottage, I see Houghton clipping the grass around the granite blocks. Coolidge races up to Houghton, her tail wagging.

I sit on Houghton's lawn near one of the blocks. "Nice day," I open.

Houghton squints at the sky, the cloud formations on the horizon. "Travelers. Rain tonight from the south." He sets his clippers on the grass. "I got something for the dog," he says. He shuffles into the house and comes back with a steak bone. Coolidge snatches it from his hands and trots happily off, lies down in the shade of a lilac bush, the bone between her forepaws.

"Houghton," I say, "you keep feeding that dog and you'll never get rid of her."

Houghton squats down, sitting on a granite block, and plants his feet apart, digs a dandelion from the lawn with his fingers. "I had a dog when I was a boy," he says. "Jeezum, I loved that dog."

"What became of him?" I ask.

"Had to get rid of him," Houghton says. "He kept digging up my mother's cotoneasters." He pronounces it "cotton easters."

"Houghton," I offer again, "I'm happy to tie the dog up."

"Heck, no," Houghton says. "A dog shouldn't be tied to a place all the time. Just keep her where she belongs, just keep her from making my rosebushes her business."

I whistle for Coolidge. "I'll see what I can do," I say although I don't think Coolidge is bothering his bushes.

I go to bed early. Houghton's lawn mower hums in the dusk. The smell of new-mown grass wafts into the room. It smells like Vermont, like my grandfather's cow barn. I inhale memories of home. Houghton's mower cuts off abruptly. I lie on the bed and let the darkness sift in over me, pearly gray. I hear the rise and fall of Coolidge's breath. She whimpers. Her feet stalk gulls in her dreams. I try to picture Cole in Newagen, tonight's destination, but I have no context for the image. I've never been there. Halyards clank against the masts of boats rocking on their moorings. The water amplifies the sound, the random chime of a clock whose works have lost the track of time. I drift. Houghton's rain arrives and drums on the tin roof. Somewhere a floorboard creaks. I feel Alison's presence in this house. How do you exorcise a memory? I wonder if Cole would consider buying a new mattress for the bed.

Coolidge wakes up before I do. She's already figured out how to open the screen door. I hear it slap into the frame. The sunlight slants into the room, feels hot and late. I yank on Alison's T-shirt and my jeans without stopping to wash my face. I see Houghton through the window methodically crumbling the soil of the flower beds in his hands, working his way down the row, inspecting the regiment of zinnias and marigolds, a bag of peat moss beside him.

When I step out on the porch, he greets me, "You people from away sure can sleep."

I stroll over, my feet crunching over the gravelly right-of-way. A tin can rests below Houghton's rosebush. "What's that?" I ask him.

"Fruit cocktail. Fermented. Got it from my sister Shirley. She says slugs go for the stuff like mad. Crawl right in and shrivel up."

"Ugh," I say. I wish I had a cup of coffee. The grass curls cold and dewy around my feet. Coolidge lopes up, her feathers wet and curly, and collapses on the grass next to me.

"I don't know how you keep a dog over there," Houghton says. "Marsh cottage isn't what you'd call roomy."

I smile. Houghton, like everyone else on the island, still calls Cole's, "Marsh cottage." Marsh owned the cottage forty-odd years and four owners ago. Houghton wipes his hands on his flannel shirt. "That place there," he says, pointing at Cole's cottage, "used to be the barn to this place. Marsh bought it from my grandmother. She owned all of this." He waves his hand vaguely over the point of land to the shore. "And that place," he gestures to a shoreside cottage, "used to be the guest cottage where we put the summercaters." He grins at me, crinkling the lines at the corners of his eyes.

I rub Coolidge's fur against the lie and wonder how many generations it takes to belong here. I part Coolidge's ruff, exposing a tick, and pluck it from her neck. "God," I say and smash the tick on a rock.

Houghton looks down at the flattened tick and asks, "Do you mind if I tell you something?" He doesn't wait for an answer, says, "I wish you wouldn't swear."

"I'm not used to them," I explain. "We don't have ticks in Vermont."

"Probably don't like it there," Houghton mutters returning to his garden, dipping his hands into the soil.

During the afternoon, I putty the window panes, take the trash to the dump, and scan the bay for the *Afterthought*. But, to me, all the sails resemble each other—linen napkins folded like tents jut into the sky from a blue tablecloth. Not a very nautical image. My ignorance embarrasses me, and I walk back to the cottage to fix some supper. Houghton waves to me from his back step where he sits shucking clams.

I sit in the wing chair in the living room reading one of Cole's *Sail* magazines. Coolidge curls up by the Franklin stove. Suddenly she starts barking, her hackles bristling. "Coolidge," I say, "it's just the wind," as the tap on the window brings her leaping up. I drop my magazine. Houghton's nose flattens against the glass, making his bespectacled face look owlish. I motion for him to come in. He wipes his feet apologetically on the doormat. "Didn't mean to give you a start," he says.

I murmur something, then gesture toward the rocker. "Have a seat."

"No thanks," Houghton says shifting his weight from foot to foot.

I look at him expectantly.

"Dog's been eating my clamshells."

"What?" I say.

"Dog's been eating my clamshells," he repeats. When I don't respond, he elucidates, "I throw the clamshells down in the driveway. Makes a good surface. Dog's been eating them."

I look at Coolidge, her ingenuous brown eyes, as if for corroboration. "Why would she . . . ?" I start and trail off. "Must be raccoons," I say.

Houghton shakes his head, his glasses sparkling in the lamp light. "Cole still sailing?" he asks looking around the room as if Cole might suddenly emerge from a shadowy corner.

"Yes," I say.

Houghton chuckles. "Once a man gets salt water in his blood . . ." He doesn't finish the thought. "Well goodnight," he says.

"Goodnight," I call out into the darkness closing in his wake like water. I snap on the porch light as Houghton's screen door slaps to. I wish Cole were home.

Before I go to bed, I look out the window. The right-of-way shimmers in the moonlight, parallel rules, nacreous with the dust of clamshells. I slap the mattress to coax Coolidge up on the bed. Her tail thumps the floor, but she doesn't rise, habituated to Cole's territorial claim to the bed. I sleep fitfully thinking I hear Cole's step on the stair. I finally fall asleep dreaming of Houghton, of what I've privately nicknamed The War of the Marigolds. I wake to a vigorous banging on the porch door, tumble out of bed and down the stairs thinking something has happened to Cole, picturing the *Afterthought* pounding against rock ledges.

"See this?" Houghton thrusts a tin can in my face. I pull my nightgown tightly around me. "Well, I'm just disgusted," Houghton sputters, "disgusted." He pauses and fumbles in his pocket, pops a nitroglycerine tablet into his mouth. "That damn dog came over and ate the slug bait. Every last dite of it." Houghton waggles the can in front of my face. He thrusts his hand into it, illustrating its emptiness. A metal gauntlet covering his wrist. Then he throws the can down on the porch floor. "Disgusted," he repeats. In the corner of my eye, I see Coolidge slink behind the rocker.

"Houghton," I say, picking up the can, "if you keep feeding the dog . . ."

"Don't give me that about feeding the dog," Houghton yells. "I've had it up to here with that goddamned dog."

He's halfway across the right-of-way before I think to shout at the back of his flannel shirt, "Houghton, I wish you wouldn't swear."

For the third day in a row, I pull on Alison's T-shirt and my jeans. As I lace up my sneakers, Coolidge wags her tail. She wriggles for attention whenever I put on my shoes, as if I might be getting ready to go home, to leave the island for Pennsylvania, or maybe Vermont, as if she feared being abandoned. "No," I say pushing her away from me. "You stay home. Stay home." Coolidge hunches into her begging pose. "No," I say and snap her muzzle with my fingers, "bad dog." She lies down and cocks one eye warily on me as I head for the stairs.

I bike to Red Dower's Island Market and pick a tin of fruit cocktail off the dusty shelf.

"No charge for the dust," Red says wiping the top of the can with his shirt cuff. I give him a dollar forty, twice what I'd pay on the mainland, and bike home.

Houghton isn't in his yard, so I leave the can, a peace offering, on the back step and wheel my bike to the cottage. I wonder if Coolidge has pawed out the screens, but, as I near, I see they are intact. As I prop the kickstand, Cole cracks the door. "Cole," I yell. He looks tan and handsome in his T-shirt speckled with the blue bottom paint of the *Afterthought.* Cole stares at my chest. He doesn't say anything. "How was it?" I ask. But Cole just stares at my chest. I've heard about mariners coming into port, lusty after shipping out, but Cole's only been gone two days.

"Carey," he says quietly, "I think you'd better go change."

I finger the neckline of my shirt, Alison's shirt. "I found it in the drawer," I say. "I didn't think it would matter."

"I think you'd better change," he says again, then starts to explain, "It's too familiar. She wore that shirt all the time. It hits a little too close to home."

"Then you should have thrown it away," I say brushing past him and clomping up the stairs. I peel the shirt off and throw it in the bathroom wastebasket. I listen for Cole's footfall, hoping he will follow me up the stairs, hoping he will come and hold me. But, from the window, I see him leaning over the mower, yanking the cord. I lie down on the unmade bed, listen to the motor sputter, then subside into a drone. Later, another mower hums, higher-pitched, Houghton's, entering its voice into the mechanical fugue. The canonical lullaby of a summer afternoon. It sings me to sleep.

Cole cracks a lobster claw and holds it over his dinner plate, draining the salt water. "The shirt just unfolded a lot of bad memories," he says. "I just want to forget the past."

I nod understandingly, although I really do not understand. How can someone forget the past, unlive his own life? I guess some people just like to tuck the past into mothballs like an old quilt; others like to keep it handy at the foot of the bed. "Well here's to the present," I say in mock toast, raising my glass of chablis.

"Here's to you," Cole says and lightly touches my forearm, so pale next to his. Coolidge pokes her nose over the edge of the table, sniffing for handouts.

While I am washing the dishes, I hear a knock on the door, then Houghton's voice say, "Evening, Cole."

"Hi Houghton."

"Give this to Carey, won't you. It's no use to me like this." The screen door bangs.

Cole comes into the kitchen, rolling a can between his palms. "What's this?" he asks.

"A can of Del Monte fruit cocktail," I say.

"Yeah, but why? What's going on?"

I recount the skirmishes of The War of the Marigolds. When I finish, Cole scratches his sunburned forearm and says, "Carey, it's a small island. You'd better watch what you say to Houghton. Houghton Bogle's been here forever; he's related to everyone."

I pull the plug in the sink. "Damn it, Cole. Do I live here or don't I? Is this my house or isn't it?" I plop the soggy dish rag into the sink. "Maybe I don't know a gunwale from an oarlock, or a Bogle from a Dower. But I can't keep tiptoeing around this island like a skeleton that snuck out of somebody's unlatched closet."

" 'Gunnel,' " Cole says.

"What?" I ask.

" 'Gunnel.' It's pronounced 'gunnel.' Nice image though, skeleton out of the closet and all that."

"Damn you. Damn this island," I say and stomp up the stairs, Coolidge close on my heels, leaving Cole laughing in the kitchen.

He is still laughing when he comes upstairs. "Can I rattle your bones?" he asks. "I have a skeleton key."

I flounce down on the bed, turn my face from Cole. Then I laugh too, feeling foolish. Cole joins me on the bed, pulls the quilt up over us. The two of us laughing under the covers in the dark. I fall asleep in his arms. No ghosts in the attic tonight.

I wake to the smell of coffee. Cole has left a pot for me on the stove. I see Houghton through the kitchen window as I pour myself a cup. When I go outside with my toolbox, Houghton doesn't look up at me. He's wedging a wire fence into the ground around the flower beds. No sign of Coolidge; she must have followed Cole down to the flats. Cole got up early to dig clams at low tide.

The sun glares through the haze. Red in the morning, sailors take warning. So hot already that I do not have to soften the glazing compound in my hands. I can hear Houghton huff just the other side of the pine trees as he bends over the roll of fencing.

I work all morning, the putty gumming my fingers, sticky as unkneaded bread dough. The patches of putty on my work shirt dry into powdery mats. I hear Houghton's mower snort into life, the crescendo-decrescendo as it traverses his lawn. Clumps of putty cling to my eyebrows, lashes. I rub my forehead and eyes, smearing more putty on my face. It's hot, I think, too hot for Cole to be digging clams, too hot for Houghton to be mowing. I'm relieved when I hear the lawnmower cut off. I set the coil of putty, all prickly with pine needles, flaked bits of paint, on the toolbox and turn toward the porch. The thought of iced coffee irresistibly lures me, drawing me like fermented fruit draws slugs . . . or dogs. I can almost feel the icy frostiness of the glass in my hand. I step from behind the pines and cast a sidelong glance to Houghton's. What I see dries my throat to dust. Houghton's legs stretch out on the grass. His right arm pokes out from underneath the mower. I cannot see his face. My legs span the right-of-way. I feel as if I'm running behind them, trying to keep up. "Oh my God," I yell. "Houghton. Oh my God."

"Jeezum," Houghton peeks out at me from underneath the mower chassis, "I wish you wouldn't swear."

"Houghton. Oh God, Houghton, I thought you were. I thought . . ."

Houghton dislodges a clod of grass from the mower with a screwdriver, then looks at me quizzically. "What got you so het up?" he asks tilting the mower higher and peering at the underbody. "You know, sometimes I'm not sure you got both your oars in the water," he says.

My legs shake. I try to find my land legs, tremble a little still as if the ground were rolling. "I saw you laid out on the grass here," I say, "and I wasn't sure. You know. Your heart."

Houghton lowers the mower to the ground, squints at me, then starts laughing. "Jeez, I was just cleaning grass off the mower," he says. "That's a corker. One month on the island, and you're ready to plant me in it. Boy that's rich," he says, trying to catch his breath between words, between laughs. "Wait 'til Shirley hears that one."

I pivot on my heel and head back to the cottage. Houghton can mow the grass until he hits soil. He can mow until he hits bedrock. He can mow until he mows this island off the continental shelf for all I care.

Cole steams clams for lunch, but I'm too hot to eat. I drink iced coffee, then lug my toolbox around to the north side of the house—the sea side. The breeze freshens. Only the picture window to glaze, and the house will be sealed tight. As I pat the putty in place with my fingers, I paraphrase Frost to myself, "I'd ask to know / What I was sealing in or sealing out . . ." Cole pauses to admire my work on his way to the shore to check on the boats. "Looking very ship-shape," he says and kisses my cheek. I wonder if he means me or the window. Coolidge naps in the tangled shadows of the raspberry bushes. "See you in a bit," Cole says and tromps off to the flapping rhythm of his hip boots. I listen to the rubbery flip-flop recede as I unloop the putty and stretch a section the length of the sill.

When I hear the approaching crunch of Houghton's boots over the clamshells, I don't turn around. I can sense him standing behind me, hear the rise and fall of his breath. Then his arm extends. His unbuttoned flannel cuff flutters like a plaid truce flag as he picks up the putty knife from the toolbox. He pinches some putty off the coil, dangles the rope of putty against the window, and strokes it expertly in place with one long, downward draw of the knife—easy as frosting a cake.

"I didn't mean to give you such a scare," Houghton says. "If the truth be known, it was darn nice of you to come running over like that." He's quiet a moment; then he says, "But Jeez, you should have seen your face." He starts laughing again at the memory. "White as a ghost in winter," he says. He chuckles. He has an irresistible chuckle like my grandfather's when he recounted one of his favorite stories—the time he had to rescue some picnicking flatlanders from the cow pasture. He loaded them like bales onto the hay wagon and towed them home with the tractor. "Even the men were screaming like old ladies," he'd tell it. "Thought the heifers were bulls." Then I'm giggling too. Houghton and I laughing together—at different stories, but that doesn't matter.

"Think that fence will keep Coolidge out of your garden?" I ask.

"Nope," Houghton says.

"Don't let it worry you, Houghton," I say. "You can't fence out something that doesn't want to be inside to begin with."

Houghton smiles, considering this, then says. "You know, I been wondering. How come you never tell me to 'Bug off, you wizzled, rimwracked old coot'?"

"That expression hasn't occurred to me, but the thought has," I say.

The blue in his eyes gleams, delighted at the thought of being told off. "Boy," he says, "I wouldn't have joked with the first one this way." He strokes the putty into place. "No sir."

"Alison?" I ask a little too quickly, then, more slowly, "What was she like?"

"Oh she was some beautiful," Houghton says, "a real keeper, as the lobstermen say."

"Oh?" I ask affecting uninterest.

"Yup," Houghton says, "she was beautiful." He pokes at the bridge of his glasses to adjust them and then adds, "But she wasn't too neighborly."

AARON'S ROD

"a token against the rebels"
Numbers 17:10

WAYNE AARON DOOLEY WAS DREADING the picnic. If he had been a clairvoyant and could have seen how the afternoon was going to fulfill itself and his dread, Wayne Dooley might have paused before he climbed into the cab with his wife, Florrie. But Wayne was not clairvoyant. He had other gifts.

The pie basket sat between them on the front seat of the pickup. Wayne Dooley snuffled. The dark maple odor signaled that Florrie was bringing the Fishes a pot of her locally famous beans. Florrie was always giving stuff away, table lamps, turkey platters, throw rugs, just handing it out free with both hands—especially since their son, Ray, had died—like she couldn't bear the property reminding her they had no heir. Wayne glanced sidelong at Florrie who hummed while she drove. Her bulky body lumped in a flowered sack of a dress, the stockings rolled around her knees like doughnuts. The plastic molded straps of her sandals, creasing like butter-knife blades into her plump feet, embarrassed him. And his embarrassment embarrassed him further, nudging him toward anger. The White family's trim women would come clucking out to the truck in their eye-smarting green and pink skirts wrapping around their sun-brown bare legs. All the White sisters wore skirts, even when they gardened, and golf socks and sneakers. Practically a family uniform. They wouldn't remark on Florrie's clothes except to extend a false compliment. They were polite, the White girls, but later they'd stretch their bare legs on the lawn and giggle about Florrie's K-Mart shift as if anybody who wore socks with pompoms poking out the heel like bunny butts had the right to cite taste violations.

"Couldn't you have worn something else?" Wayne snapped.

Florrie stopped humming. She shook the white pigtail curls of her perm. "You sure got a hair across it today. What's making you so grouchy?"

"Like you don't know. Those Fish people are just summoning us up to their picnic for a spot of local color. We're the sideshow, Florrie. Soon's I get out of the truck they'll start talking like the mercury in their I.Q. thermometers just dropped forty degrees and they all contracted contagious monosyllabism. 'Yup,' they'll say, and 'How's it hangin', Rufus?' "

Florrie laughed the genial, throaty laugh Wayne liked. The truck bumped up the dirt road. "The White girls just want someone to help them find a good spot to sink a well for the new guest house. You know that. And you, Wayne Dooley, just happen to be the best dowser in town."

"Yeah," Wayne said, "and behind my back they'll all be rolling their eyes and poking each other and asking me what my astrological sign is and how long Shirley MacLaine and me been attending the same coven." He took off his cap and crunched it in his hand.

"Whew. You're ugly today. Why, Wayne Aaron Dooley, you've known the White girls for half a century now. Meg and Mary are as common-sense people as you can meet." The truck crested the hill.

Wayne popped his cap back on his head and lowered the bill over his eyes. "They don't belong," he mumbled.

"Whites," Florrie blurted. "Why there been Whites or Sawyers in Dooley Four Corners for years and years."

"Summer people," Wayne countered.

"Far back as we remember, maybe. But Whites are cousins to Sawyers, and Sawyers have been in Vermont six generations, long as Dooleys. And somewhere back there they were year-round." Florrie eased up on the accelerator as she negotiated the curve.

"Close only counts in horseshoes," Wayne said, then added, "Damn, this road's washboarded. Why don't the Fishes with all their money throw a little into the road? Have to get the front end realigned just so we can get there." He fell quiet a minute, feeling mean. Florrie loved parties, even parties with the mucky-muck. He glowed when people praised her beans or pies. Good-natured, Florrie was, unselfconscious and chatty. Good-natured or stone-stupid coming as she did from the most inbred family in the county. Not like Dooleys. Dooleys' bloodlines ran as clear as brook water. And Dooleys had been in Vermont since forever. Dooleys belonged. His grandfather, Aaron Dooley, used to say that when the glaciers pushed down from Canada, Dooleys pushed back.

Florrie hummed over the engine drone and metallic jounce of the truck. Shocks shot to hell.

Florrie said, "You'd better treat them nice when we get there. Whites got a right to be here, too."

"Maybe the Whites do," Wayne said. "But who the hell is this Fish?"

"Mary's been married to Carl Fish for almost twenty years now." Florrie shook her head. "You can't blame a woman for marrying, Wayne. Look what I married." She grinned at him.

He scowled back. "Maybe so. But you can bet there's no one pushing up field stones in the Sawyer-White family graveyard under the name Fish. Only Sawyers and Whites buried at the old Sawyer farm. This Fish character's from away. And I can blame him for coming out and squealing, 'Howdy,' like we're the cartoon pigs dancing in from the *Hee Haw* stage set. And then he'll slight himself as an 'out-a-stater' and 'summer folk' just to show me that he understands how we locals see them."

"He's just trying to let you know he's regular," Florrie said.

"And he's not," Wayne muttered.

"Well, you just remember to be nice," Florrie said, pulling up neatly by the garage and stretching the smile she reserved for social occasions across her face.

"Howdy, hi ya, hi ya, hi ya." Carl Fish blustered out of the house, waving the stub of his cigarette in his hand.

Wayne thought Carl Fish was the jitteriest man he'd ever set eyes on. He probably smoked in his sleep. Mr. Fish approached the truck. "Come on out," he yelled. "Join the party." Carl Fish hesitated for a moment, looking at his cigarette, then flicked it onto the driveway, a good-ol'-boy gesture Wayne guessed was staged just for him, given the absence of any other butts in the driveway. "Good to see ya, good to see ya," Carl said.

"Hi, Carl," Wayne said, leaning slowly into the door as he opened it. He shifted his weight, lowered himself one leg at a time as if his limbs operated on some intricate and obsolete pulley system.

"Hey, hey. There's a keg of beer up on the patio." Carl nudged him with his elbow.

Wayne looked up at the terrace. "Sure enough," he said.

Florrie had already bounded from the cab and toted her basket of beans up the stairs. She was making nice with the ladies, flitting around the lawn furniture, stacking paper plates, spreading napkins. Sure enough, Wayne noted, Mary White Fish had on one of her screamer green skirts, this one hemmed with a border of wood ducks bill-to-tail like the moving targets in the state fair shooting booth.

"Get you a long, tall frosty one, eh?" Carl asked.

"No, I think I'll get right to the dowsing, if you don't mind," Wayne said.

Carl bounced from foot to foot. "Then, hey, let me call the boys. They wouldn't miss this for anything. They're pretty excited. Hey Chipster, Donny boy, Wayne Dooley's here to do some dowsing. Come on down."

Wayne watched the two boys unfold themselves from their lawn chairs. They could be lawn furniture themselves, the way they rose, me-thodical, hinges easing their joints into place. The two boys approached, moving with the loose-jointed, who-gives-a-shit cool of teenagers that Wayne remembered from his own boy, Ray, at about fifteen.

"They don't look too excited," Wayne said just low enough so Mr. Fish wouldn't be sure if he'd heard it.

Wayne headed for a crabapple tree, removed his pocket knife and selected a slender, crotched sapling branch, notched it, snapped it, smoothed it with two neat strokes of the blade, then peeled the bark from the leg of the Y.

"Hey, hey boys. Come watch this. You might learn something from a real Vermonter. 'Grade A' Vermonter. Heh heh."

Wayne heard the boys shuffling toward Carl. He looked up. Carl was patting his pockets for cigarettes. His disappointed hands plucked a leaf from a tree and started deveining it.

The taller boy, Chip, leaned in slightly toward Wayne. "What you doing?" he asked.

"Fixing a dowsing stick," Wayne answered. "Fruit trees are best. Flexible." He tested the forked branch by holding it out before him, then took a step forward, flexing the branch lightly. "This'll do," Wayne said, and he started shambling forward in what Florrie called his dowser's polka; step, step, shuffle, stop. "Here," he said, looking over his shoulder at Carl. "Here would be okay." Step, step, shuffle, stop. "And here." Step. "And here. A lot of water up here, and not running too deep, either." He poked his stick out ahead of him.

"Like riding a trike," one of the Fish boys said. The other snickered. Wayne turned and glared at them. Punks, just like Ray was at their age. Only these two punks were still alive. Jesus, sometimes he wondered if God didn't deal from the bottom of the deck. Black flies nettled and vexed his face. He swiped at his brow with the back of his hand. What the hell was he doing here on a perfectly fine June afternoon, strutting like a midway freak for two pimply punks? He turned his eyes to Carl. "How close to the new building do you want the well?" he asked.

"Dad, I'm gonna go get a beer," Chip said, sticking his hip out like a dare.

"Hey, no, Chipster. Slow down," Carl Fish said. "Why don't you just give this dowsing a try? Can they give it a try? Just give it a try, boys." Carl's hands whirled like pinwheels. His forehead ran in little streams. He was sweating for a cigarette. Carl lifted his brows, pleading. "What d'you say?"

"Yup. They can give it a try." Wayne tossed his dowsing stick aside and scanned the edge of the field. Chokecherry. Even these two jokers could feel the tug of a chokecherry. As he cut the new sticks, he could feel the boys' skepticism rising from them like morning fog from the river. They were just humoring him. He'd show them water. He hacked the tender bark from the pale green wood. He tossed the first stick back, then the second. The boys picked up the sticks and swung them carelessly with that odd mix of self-consciousness and arrogance peculiar to adolescent boys, reminding Wayne again of Ray, that last day Wayne had seen him alive, sixteen years old and twirling his car keys on his finger like a Hollywood cowboy with an itchy trigger finger. "Shit," Wayne cursed.

"Not like that. Hold them out in front of you, firm but with a light touch."

The boys perked up when Wayne said "shit," but as he issued directions, they eyed each other dubiously. The younger one's cheeks bulged and reddened with the laugh he choked back.

"Well move, damn it," Wayne ordered. "The water's not going to come to you."

The boys stepped forward uncertainly, coltish. Carl shredded another leaf. Regular mulcher, that Carl. His nicotine-stained finger turned green with chlorophyll.

"You feel anything?" Chip asked aside to Donald.

"You?" Donald asked back.

"Not if you didn't," Chip said.

"I didn't," Donald said.

"Keep moving," Wayne commanded. He could hear Mary's chatter preceding her as the ladies approached across the lawn.

"Why you dear, sweet man," Mary sang. "So sweet of you to involve the boys like that." She pecked Wayne's cheek.

Florrie stiffened. Kissing was going some even for Florrie. Wayne turned his head away and retreated a step from Mary.

"Mary's been telling me how the boys hope to make bachelors' quarters out in the guest house once the new water's hooked up," Florrie said.

Wayne squinted in the direction of the boys, and nodded to indicate he'd heard Florrie.

"Of course with them on their own out there we'll have to watch them like mother hens," Mary said, "for girls and b-e-e-r."

Wayne stifled a laugh, wondering on whose behalf the woman was so protectively spelling. Florrie? Himself? He glanced at Carl.

Carl nodded. "B-e-e-r," he repeated solemnly and sprinkled his frazzled leaf on the grass like confetti, "beer."

"Shit, I'm not a moron," Wayne said and kicked his boot at a hillock of grass. "I can spell 'beer.' " He knew beer all right. Ray had tanked up his rebuilt Willys, then himself, and drove the jeep halfway up an elm by Bates Bridge. They found the body in the river.

"Hey. I felt something," Chip screamed with excitement.

"Yeah. Yeah. Me too." Donald flung his stick wide aside like he'd handled a snake. The two boys ran panting back to the group on the lawn.

"You should feel it, Dad. That sucker just curled right down."

"Mine damn near snapped right off."

"Mine jumped right out of my hands. You ought to try it."

They talked over each other in their excitement. Wayne's mouth twisted into a wry premonition of a smile, so mere only Florrie would notice.

Chip recovered first. "Yeah. Well, you know. It's okay. Semi-cool." He averted his eyes from Wayne. "You ought to try it sometime, Dad."

"Yeah, it's pretty cool," Donald mimicked his brother's understatement.

"Hell, let me at it." Carl scooped Wayne's dowsing stick from the grass. "You mind, Wayne?"

"Nope." Wayne wondered how Carl's fidgety hands would ever recognize a tremble of the rod.

The afternoon passed with the ladies passing plates and clearing plates and chatting and insinuating until they got down to full-hearted gossiping, and with the boys and men eating potato salad and beans and cold cuts and drinking beer and strolling around the field, holding out their dowsing sticks, and drinking more beer, and stumbling around the field, holding their sticks and cracking raw jokes about whose stick was the longest. And Wayne relieved himself in the chokecherries, thinking, as he zipped up, that Carl Fish wasn't half-bad, but maybe it was just the beer because anybody looked better through the bottom of a drained glass.

And then he thought maybe it wasn't the beer when Carl started clapping him on the back, powdering him with cigarette ash and compliments, slurring, "You're a genius, Wayne. A pure and simple genius. You got a gift. I'm telling you. You're a regular water witch."

And later, after his remorse and hangover wore off, Wayne would decide to blame it on the beer, thinking the tree never did grow far from the acorn, and that, just like Ray, he got full of himself when he got full of beer and the high regard of other men. He couldn't rewind time like a wristwatch. He had done what he had done, and Florrie had been the first to see it coming, but once he got started, he couldn't help himself. It was like trying to arrest a force of nature, evaporate a deluge with a disposable lighter. Once Wayne got the flow going, he couldn't close the tap.

Carl kept saying he wanted the well near the new guest house, which was only a few yards from the old Sawyer family cemetery. "Hey, hey, surely a real Vermonter like yourself can find water over by the new bachelors' quarters, eh?" Carl urged him on, brandishing his cigarette like a cattle prod. "Surely you real Vermonters can tap into the ground easy as you tap into a sugar maple, eh? Eh? No?" He sounded like somebody doing a bad impersonation of Tom Poston doing George Utley doing a bad impersonation of a third-generation-Vermont French Canadian. "Darn tooting, a real Vermonter'll find water in these hills, eh? Eh? No?"

And Wayne said, "You want water, I'll give you water okay." And he'd thrashed out into the hardhack and into the woods, hauling back some windfall, crotched and half-rotted, thick as a log, and gleaming with phosphorus. And Carl, drunk, hooted and fell all over his older boy, drunk, and the younger, who pretended to be, as Wayne, drunk, half-crouched and hefted the log up into his lap. Even as dusky as it was growing and from halfway across the yard, Florrie saw the green in Wayne's eyes gleam, spark, brighten to match the log's phosphorescence. "No," she hollered. "Wayne, don't."

But it was too late. Wayne felt young and green as wet well-moss. His arms grew strong as timbers. He cocked the log firm against his abdomen. Erect, the log thrust into the sky. Wayne, straining from the effort, trickled, then ran, then soaked with sweat. He threw back his head and laughed a laugh that popped his cap off and rumbled through the ground.

He could sense the water seeping, trickling, through granite crevices, pulsing, rushing, gushing, and reversing grade in unseen aquifers. The water thrummed in his veins, drummed in his temples. "No," Florrie shrieked again. But he stood his ground, focused his energy like a conduit. Once, he glanced at Carl, whose color was draining as if it, too, were being sucked up into the vortex of Wayne's concentration. Wayne blinked at the image of Carl and his two handsome boys, their handsome house, handsomely decorated by the handsome White woman. And he felt as if he could suck it all up, the whole farm and fam-damily, pull them into the ground, percolate them through the groundwater beds and up through layers of rock and earth, and spurt them out, spray them all over the rugged face of the state in a mist. Vaporize them.

His hands shook on the log. The turf around him mounded, bubbled, and then the water spurted out, gushing ever higher and higher into a geyser on a spume of rainbows in the late afternoon sun. The briefest hope flashed in Wayne; he wished Ray could have seen it. But the water dashed the thought aside, fluming up in a gravity-defying cascade. Wayne should have stopped there. And he would have if he had known what was coming next. The water spiked up by the dowser log as if Wayne extended a magic wand. And Wayne himself would have been hard pressed to say whether the water leapt at or from the log. But even in his elation he knew he would never be able to conjure up that much power again.

And then it happened. First, a single bone appeared in the spout of water, then another. Then whole skeletons appeared, rising from the graveyard in the spout of water, and, before their eyes, some of the stray bones assembled into skeletons, and the skeletons grew flesh and hair and even clothing. And old man Sawyer, floundering in his nightshirt, burbled and motored his old chicken legs like he was treading water, blinking and snapping his head around to find the son of a bitch who'd awakened him. And beneath him, his fat wife Angie rolled like a doughnut in a kettle of bubbling lard with her children bobbing around her like doughnut holes. And Wayne thought he heard old man Sawyer, his eye sockets locked on Wayne's, gargling something about his grandfather, taking poor old Aaron Dooley's name in vain.

"Holy cow," Carl Fish said, whistled low, then asked, "What is that?"

"That," Wayne Dooley said, "why that, Carl, is real Vermonters."

Then Wayne lost his grip of the mossy log, fumbled it, and blacked out. The rest of the story Wayne pieced together from Florrie's angry spluttering. As soon as he dropped the log, the water vanished. The mound muddied into a little puddle. The grass nearby wasn't even wet. Old man Sawyer faded as abruptly as the rainbows riding the spray.

Florrie found Wayne's cap in the grass and wrung it out on his face. She ushered him to the truck, muttering the whole way. "You had to show off, didn't you. You couldn't leave well enough alone. The whole town's going to hear about this one. You just better hope the Fishes say it was a group case of pink elephants. You're blessed with a gift like that and you squander it at a picnic. Well," she said, "I hope you're proud of yourself. Now they'll never invite us back." And when she'd had her say, she fell black and silent as a moonless night in January.

Wayne felt pretty bad at first, thinking of old man Sawyer's bones leaching all those years, dissolving peacefully into the groundwater before he came along and treated the man's remains like something to squirt on a vegetable garden. And he felt bad, too, thinking he had dribbled away the power he might have used to baptize Ray anew. But he didn't think he could have borne parting with his son twice. Perhaps it all had occurred as it should have. And once the hangover receded, he realized that he was, indeed, pretty proud of himself. No transplanted dowser could have done what he did. Nope. Only a native could summon that much sympathy from the ground. It would be a long time before Florrie spoke to him again. But a man twice-blessed should not complain.

THE TEN JOYFUL MYSTERIES
OF THE ONE TRUE FAITH

WE WERE BAD CATHOLICS, irredeemably bad. On Fridays, we complained about the tuna noodle hot dish and its mystery ingredient—potato chips? Corn flakes? On Saturdays, my brother Danny and I lined up outside the convent to be herded inside with the other part-time Catholics to be catechized. On Sundays, we attended church but squeezed into the back pew, my father in the aisle seat, so he could lead the stampede after Communion to beat the post-Benediction press and be the first to peel out of the parking lot in his flowered Willys jeep ahead of the more solemn family cars, the station wagons and sedate sedans.

No rosary beads clicked in our house. No votive candles flickered. No blue-eyed statuettes collected dust on their Ginny doll eyelashes and gilt-trimmed gowns. We remembered the Holy Days unless we forgot. We were generous with the collection plate but stingy with our souls. We were, as Genella down the street sensed, convertible. And she tried mightily to sway us, to lead us astray from the school of Mackerel-Snappers, in the small French-Canadian town to which we'd recently moved and over which the hilltop Baptist Church prevailed.

Genella lived in an apartment that had no plumbing, in the rowhouse across from the defunct woolen mill. A hand pump in the kitchen equipped the Laleekes with the ability if not the proclivity to wash dishes and clothes. The Laleekes descended the rickety wooden steps to the dirt cellar to relieve themselves in facilities Danny and I strained to imagine.

"Do you suppose they pee on the dirt floor?"

"Or a chamber pot or an indoor privy?"

101

It was a mystery my mother determined would remain arcane. She forbade us to step beyond the front room, which, either Genella smelled like, or which smelled like Genella—sweat, and molding plaster, unwashed shifts, and last week's boiled dinners—the incense she wafted as she pronounced us damned, because in the Baptist white-clapboarded eyes of the small Maine town, we were, to a Mac-Snap worshipper, idolaters.

Genella, shapeless and ageless, her hair a reliquary of unwashed ringlets, derived, in the dim Acadian past, from Catholic stock, devout until some suggestible forebear relocated his household and faith to Maine. She presented a persuasive, hefty authority that could have been ecumenical if the bulk of her ideas and body had not been so thoroughly indoctrinated with Baptism. Living in near-darkness on a diet of cheese curls and orange soda, she and her mother shared the orange complexion of the fat my mother scraped from chicken breasts on the permissible meat days.

In Catechism, Sister Marie Francine told us we were damned to hellfire if we didn't believe in the One True Faith. In her stuffy apartment, Baptist Genella told us we were damned to hellfire if we did, this contradiction making faith, already well-prickered for a seven- and a nine-year-old, a thorny issue.

Augmenting our religious confusion, the Latin mass frequently lapsed into the regional hybrid that grafted a French scion onto a branch of regional English. Sunday after Sunday, Danny and I endured the mumbo-jumbo of the mystery play, goggle-eyed and half-glimpsed through a nodding field of ambitious hats: veiled mink pillboxes, black dotted 1960s patent-leather domes, broad-brimmed Breakfast at Tiffany's toppers that rivaled, even challenged to outshine, any bishop's miter. We suppressed hat-induced giggles. We knelt, we chanted, we recanted with only the slimmest sliver of comprehension of our roles in the symbolic re-enactment, slimmer than the papery hosts glued to the roofs of our mouths, as we waited until my father elbowed aside our devotion and my mother who yanked Danny who yanked me from the pew in a Rube Goldbergian mechanism, my mother apologetically splashing holy water on the two of us and the sand-ground floor as we exited, following my father on his pilgrimage to Captain Billy's for the Sunday *Times.*

The Cap stoutly, grimly, sadistically refused to hold the *Times* for any man—with no bias as to profession, rank, economic standing, or regularity of purchasing habit, a policy he communicated with no English at all but with the grunts and economical hand gestures of his native hybrid French. He was, as my father habitually said with pleasure at my mother's displeasure, a bastard. A dyed-in-la-laine bastard. When unaccompanied by my father, my brother and I avoided the Captain.

We could not avoid the nuns. The mumbling nuns in their shapeless habits, their only observable utilitarian body parts being the hard-as-iron, leather-clad toes clicking beneath their hems, inspired a particular awe that verged on terror. Their black habits pinned cloth to cloth, or perhaps, like the "Little Flower's," cloth to grateful, penitential skin, their hands obscured, their rosaries dangling, their faces attached to the rimless spectacles their noses precipitously supported, their brows half-haloed with paper plates, they trundled unimpeded, respected, even feared on our sidewalks. Traffic lights changed for them. Logging trucks squealed to halts. Incorrigible cursers idling in Captain Billy's or at the soda fountain inflated with their swallowed execrations like cows' bellies distended with unexpulsed grass-gas until the nuns exited and the cursers rumbled free. A mystery of religious tolerance, even Baptists stepped aside on our sidewalks to let nuns pass. The sisters had the power.

Mother Superior, who possessed an authority that apparently transcended name-bearing, raised the deepest, darkest, paranoid fantasies as easily as she raised her oak ruler to the wayward hand of the offspring of a Diocesan parent who, dwelling in ignorance, still had not enrolled his charges in the parochial school and her remedial instruction, but chose, instead, to catechize them weekly and weakly. My parents were such parents. And their neglect turned fertile soil for a Baptist proselytizer's seed.

"They shave their heads," Genella catechized us in her parlor. "And they marry Christ. My mother says it's a polygamy of virgin brides, and you know what that means: S-E-X," she said with a lewd arch of her well-larded eyebrows.

And we nodded gravely, sex being as immense a mystery as any other to us, understood only as that conversational shove that shooed us from the lap of the living room during "Grownup Hour" and that rocked my parents' cocktail parties with laughter. An "in" joke. But we intuited. Forbidden fruit nags a sweet tooth. And Danny sank his into a recommended sex-ed. text in the library that illustrated the sweet mystery of life with cows' uteri and that he charged all his nail-biting, nose-picking friends in the neighborhood 25¢ to see until a vigilant mother confronted my heretofore blinkered mother, who put an end to Danny's budding entrepreneurship.

Danny took it in stride, running through the milkweed jungle of our backyard, throwing stones at the broken windows in the abandoned mill, daring me to high-wire walk the width of the concrete hydraulic dam, grinding elderberries into his prepubescent beloved's T-shirts, whom, when she complained about the stains, we shoved into the shallows of the Mousam River, love another mystery that immersed us in violent and sopping wet confusion.

When we were not raising H-E-double-hockey-sticks, we diverted ourselves on the long walks back from Lincoln School raising our spirits and voices trying to raise Genella's ire with this litany:

> Fatty, Fatty two-by-four
> Couldn't get through the bathroom door,
> So she did it on the floor,
> Fatty, Fatty, two-by-four.

This amused us until Danny, ever the empiricist, pragmatically pointed out that Genella had no bathroom floor, and, limited by the literalism of our imaginations and frustrated by our inability to rhyme other cruelties, we contented ourselves with the occasional Genella-trailing, half-hearted cry of "Hey Fatso" or "Hey Tubby."

Genella laughed it off, jiggling in her protective layers. Her flesh was her bodyguard. Like the nuns, she had the upper hand, and she knew it. She was older than we were; Genella knew things. How she knew things remained a mystery, but she patted deep in her muumuu pocket the key that unlocked the secrets of convent life. She knew we could never ostracize her; we'd always come back for more.

Spreading over her overstuffed easy chair in her stinky front room, her ankle-socked feet daintily crossed, she tempted us with the teaser, "The nuns travel in pairs, because they dress and undress each other. Too many pins to manage alone."

I scooted forward at this, being recently troubled by the omnipresence of my guardian angel. Was he "ever this day at my side," for example, when I stripped to put on my clown pajamas? Was he "ever at my side" when I bathed? I was naturally modest, so Genella had my attention if not yet Danny's. But she snared him when, after a pause, she divulged, "And they sleep in their coffins at night."

Danny inhaled sharply the air of radiator-dried musty mittens, of linoleum tar gumming up the daily dirt scuffed in by years of converted Laleekes. "No," he said and scoffed. "You're thinking of Count Dracula. 'I vant to bite you in ze neck.' "

But, smug in her fat and conviction, Genella settled. It was like arguing with gravity. Danny couldn't get a rise out of her. "They sleep in their coffins," Genella repeated.

Outside, Danny said, "No. No coffins," as we scuffled home through a sidewalk trough of crackly leaves in a darkness particular to Maine autumnal nights, an early evening pitch as black as habits. "I don't believe it; do you?"

A frosty halo gleamed around the moon. "No," I echoed, "I don't believe it." But I weakened. "Genella knows things, though, things Mom and Dad don't even know."

"Like what?"

"Like she told you about the cow-book in the library that made you a heap of money and trouble."

Danny walked beside me silently, and then I sang, "I know an old lady who swallowed a cow. I don't know how she swallowed a cow," just to provoke him to throw an armful of leaves at me, which he did, and then he ran like the devil and I pursued him like one of Satan's own upstart minions. We whirled down the street like dry leaves. He winded me and beat me home. Danny and I both knew he was fast and wiry, but I was wily. I whiled my time, knowing that Danny would have to verify that nuns sleep in their coffins, knowing that it would come to this: a dare to sneak out at night, to creep out to the laundry porch after dinner, to lower ourselves hand under hand on the rope swing, to daredevil step-by-step across the dam, to cut through the weedy mill parking lot, to steam down a length of railroad ties, to scramble up the hill to the yellow peeping rectangles of light in the convent windows. So we avoided each other, he, galloping around with the dementos in his

Mad Scientist Club, me and my friends arranging plastic improbable sex scenes with our Ken and Barbie dolls that the Kinseys wouldn't have a statistical whim how to decipher.

For a week, we kept busy avoiding each other. Then it snowed. Snow glazed the inevitable with icy danger, lured us with the trackable threat of discovery. We couldn't resist. After dinner, we reconnoitered and assembled our gear of mittens, woolen hats, jackets, and plausible lies. We settled on rolling snowmen as a wholesome activity my mother would condone. And she obliged.

The night sky vainly strove to shroud the yellow tinge that the snowstorm cast. The moon shivered inside a silver aureole silvering an already silvery world with shimmery light. We scuffed along the hidden sidewalks, deluded we were breaking trails through virgin landscapes only to discover the marks of those who'd braved the elements before us. In front of Genella's rowhouse, beneath a cone of streetlight, someone had written in the snow: Ringo, John, George, and Paul. We couldn't tolerate the arrogance of these neighborhood invaders, kids whose names were a mystery to us and, no doubt, not a Catholic among them, so we added our names, Joan and Dan, spelling them out in the drift with a snapped branch of Mrs. Emory's prized rhododendron, which had defied climate and nature and naturalized. Satisfied, we pushed on, dropping down into the dark shadow of the mill, ice-walking across the dam, bumping over the ties and up the hill to the lip of the church lot.

Among nuns' supernatural powers was the ability to summon snow-plows. The parking lot glistened clear and wet in reflected moonlight, walled by banks of perfectly packed snow, a tarmac apron to the convent.

"Dare you."

"Dare you."

"Dared you first."

"Dared you first."

"Liar, liar, pants on fire."

"I'm rubber; you're glue. Bounces off me and sticks to you."

Exhausted by the volley, we slid down the snowbank and crept in tandem to the windows, I, now a well-photographed Soldier in Christ's Army, Danny, an equally well-photographed First Communicant. We reached the sidewalk that wrapped around the convent. Ducking, we hunched into the shadow and hugged its brick wall. We were both breathing loudly enough to make the other self-conscious, and I pretended not to notice as Danny gulped air to regulate his breathing, hoping for a similar courtesy. We trembled together beneath the window ledge envisioning—I'm sure jointly—Jungian images, black-winged harpies, their sacred hearts dripping blood, their white headpieces splattered with drops from their gouged, thorn-crowned foreheads, their bodies flapping from their coffins in a squealing sonar bat-wing flurry to sink their teeth into our impure necks from which dangled no scapulars, no saints' medals, no protective crosses against our sins and their bald heads catapulting, pummelling us roundly like the dreadful crossfire of a satisfying snowball fight.

"Ladies first," Danny said, his politeness a huffy fog in the cold, moist air.

"Youth before beauty," I puffed back.

We both intuited that if ever there was a mortal sin, our imminent spying on nuns was it. But we had to honor the dare. In states of disgrace, we raised our heads, found ourselves peeping at two old nuns, Sisters Thérèse and Jeanne, who were contemplating wooden disks on bingo cards between them. I started to laugh then, scorning our fear, which was only just beginning to ebb, when before our eyes, it happened. A miracle. A horror. The nuns transubstantiated into black, alar furies. The cards and disks blew away before their dervish force, their otherworldly shrieks conjuring up the head harpy—the hulking black avatar of our deepest anticipatory fears: Mother Superior's black bulk materialized from nowhere, her whiskery mouth zooming in close-up and booming through the cracked "pour-bonne-santé" window, "Les voyeurs. Intolérable! Au secours. Police. Prêtre. Eek. Eek. Eek," she squeaked.

Her volume knocked us back breathless from the window. We gathered ourselves, scattered and scampered, slid into the merciless wall of the parking lot, scaled its icy scarp, skated on our spines down the crusty crest of snow, and landed at the base of the mound knee-deep in the fluff, our hearts pounding with the zeal of the newly converted, Genella's mission fully realized—but obliquely.

Awestruck, baptized in snow and moonlight, we'd seen the light, and we had been transformed. In a single evening, we'd developed an instinct for the respectful distance to maintain from a mystery. Despite our former doubts, it was true. We'd seen it with our own eyes. We'd never thought the nuns were human, but we'd never imagined that Mother Superior was really a bat. Danny and I couldn't talk to each other about what we'd seen. Well-doused in snow, piety, and fear, our credulity transformed to credo, we believed. The vision may have been a communal hallucination, either religious or imaginative, but it hardly mattered which. We had been licked, licked kitten clean, by the cat-rough tongue of faith. We'd never be convertible again.

A HARD PLACE

WHEN I LIVED IN VERMONT, I used to meet Sabra for coffee at a diner, The Rustic Roost, outside Bethel. The Roost was a converted chicken coop with a concrete floor, chrome and red vinyl chairs, and fifties' Formica tables. Natives insisted that on wet days they could still whiff the chicken droppings. But I smelled only the chicory-bitter, warm brown of coffee steam, the bacon grease of the grill, the bubbly oil slick of the deep fryer.

While I waited for Sabra, I chatted with Emmy, a waitress in her fifties who had raised four kids alone. Sometimes Sabra ran late, the trip from Hanover lengthened by a meeting or by the rain, sleet, ice, and snow storms that were typical but not predictable.

"Sabra late?" Emmy would ask.

I'd nod. "Her meeting must have run over again."

Emmy might tuck her pencil behind her ear, or pat her French twist. "She's the meetingest person I ever knew," she'd say.

From my conversations with Emmy over two years, I learned: that she'd always lived in Vermont; she had a passion for moose and was delighted that the state herd was growing, but couldn't care less about deer; that when her husband, Ray, punched her, she decked him and kicked him out; that he was sober now and married to another AA member in Rutland who had a bad dye job; that she had three boys and one girl, all grown now, and her only brother, who lived in New York state, had recently died.

Since Emmy served me these biographical side dishes with the free refills promised in the window sign, I offered her the rough outline of my life: I'd moved to Vermont to be near my former boyfriend only to learn proximity didn't close the gap. We'd split up after a few months of half-hearted intimacy. He was a yarn-dyed, buffalo-plaid Woodchuck who would never leave Vermont. By constitution and conditioning, I was a traveler. My father, a restless professor who believed the next job, the next place, would always be better than the previous one, had relocated the family every two years, that being the lifespan of his idealism, successively disappointed. For a year, I'd assisted a Dartmouth professor on a dig of a stone structure he hoped was a Viking ruin. But locals, who called it the Troll Hole, claimed it was just an old ice house. The job expired at year's end, and I was already looking for another job. And my friend Sabra, also an academic's daughter, was a college friend, an art major currently working as a museum curator at Dartmouth. These were the details I offered Emmy across the bar.

One day during a busy lunch hour, Sabra sat at the counter, toying with the tassels of her plum-colored scarf. "Do you have a heart place?" she asked.

"A heart place?" I echoed, glancing at the coveralled coffee drinker to Sabra's right who squinted at her, head cocked as he fished a cigarette from his pack.

"You know," Sabra said, "some foreign landscape, never visited, that mysteriously, mystically summons you. I am certain Tibet is calling me." The fringe of her scarf wriggled on the worn boomerang pattern of the counter. The coffee-drinker lit his cigarette, and Sabra waved off his smoke with a flourish of her scarf.

"Heart place," I said. "I don't know; I've always wanted to visit the Yucatan."

"Visit?" Sabra asked, her dark eyes narrowing. "I'm talking about finding your spiritual home, your soul's nest, the heart place."

The coffee-drinker spun a quarter-turn on his stool.

I averted my eyes from him and watched Emmy scrape the grill. "Soul's nest? I don't know. The Yucatan has always intrigued me."

Sabra emptied a sugar packet into her mug and asked, "Is the Yucatan your heart place?"

I looked up as Emmy, buttering an English muffin, interrupted, "I've been some hard places, I can tell you. And I don't feel the need to go to any more of them."

The coffee-drinker thumped down his mug. Sabra laughed. "Not 'hard place,' *heart place.* Some place you've never been to, but you've always wanted to go. Only, it's more than that. It's almost as if you feel you're supposed to go there. You're destined."

Sabra's neighbor tucked his cigarettes into his bib pocket, muttered, "I got me a heart place." He thumped the patch pocket. "My chest." As the man spun to leave, Sabra rolled her eyes.

Beside her, the split vinyl of the vacated stool twirled lazily.

"Don't mind Red," Emmy said, pointing her butter knife at his back. "Nobody gets his jokes."

I creased my napkin and asked, "Have you ever longed to go some-place special, Emmy, someplace you've never seen?"

"Yes." She set down the plate on the counter. She leaned forward, her eyes the blue of a match-flare's center, her hands flattened on the Formica. Sabra set down her cup and stared as Emmy said in a plaintive voice, "Yes, there's a place like that, a place I always wanted to go. I've always dreamed about going to Schenectady, New York."

I snapped my head, staring furiously at Sabra: do not laugh. Please, do not laugh at this woman. Grateful that Sabra did not have a swallow of coffee in her mouth, which I could imagine spattering the white front of Emmy's uniform.

Keeping my tone even, I asked, "Why Schenectady?"

"My brother Paul who passed away lived there. He made it sound so grand." Emmy shook her head, then grabbed the coffee pot from the burner behind her and worked her way down the counter, pouring and chatting.

Red-faced with suppressed laughter, Sabra grabbed my hand and squeezed it hard. "Schenectady. Can you believe? I used to live in Schenectady when my father taught at Union. Why would anyone want to go there?"

I shook my head, but over the upcoming weeks as I waited for Sabra, I found out. Having cracked the binding on Schenectady, Emmy had many pages of Paul's description to rustle.

"There's Proctor's Arcade and inside the arcade, Proctor's Theater. All the seats are red velvet, not just the opera boxes. Brocade covers the walls. The brass railings gleam. A chandelier dangles real crystal drops." Here Emmy would pause before resuming.

"And not just one theater—two. There's a State Street Theater which is almost as nice. And where Erie Boulevard runs there are watermarks on the corner restaurant where the canal used to flood. And storefronts line Jay Street where dealers sell old crank Victrolas and antique postcards. Near the arcade, a Planter's Peanuts roasts peanuts daily. The whole street smells toasty with them. And behind the arcade, sits a red store where they grind coffee in big red enamel grinders with brass wheels. And they sell tea, too, not just everyday tea, but orange tea and spice tea and sticks of incense, bundled in red papers and the whole room smells fresh and well . . ." Unable to convey the aroma, Emmy threw up her arms, palms extended.

But I found myself smelling the peanuts and coffee. And I imagined another scene as well: the brother Paul arriving by train. Snowdrifts mounded everywhere. Emmy and her mother stuffing a turkey on the kitchen table, wiping their hands on their aprons, talking animatedly. Paul unpacking upstairs in the unheated bedroom with flowered wallpaper, a corner discolored by a brown heart-shaped watermark where ice built up in the eaves during a blizzard two decades ago. The kitchen chatter rises to him with the stove heat through the curlicued iron grate in the floor. A wet snow slops the window. He unpacks his leather valise. He hates it here. Claustrophobic already, he goes downstairs with his parcels: the red-wrapped sticks of incense, the Victorian valentine postcards with some stranger's spidery script on the back, the foil packets of loose tea with bits of orange rind and clove, the paper sacks of peanuts, which his mother and sister unwrap as if they were marvels. And he tells them about movies he's seen in the Proctor Theater and plays and concerts he's heard. And they, who watch Lawrence Welk on Saturday nights and drive to West Lebanon to shop, shake their heads.

"Emmy's got me," I told Sabra over coffee. "I'm starting to imagine Schenectady." I recounted Emmy's description.

Sabra wrapped her purple silk neck scarf around her hand like a bandage, and stared at me with her brown, full-fringed eyes. "You poor dear. It isn't like that, at least not anymore. I grew up there. It was a G.E. town. Streets of duplexes, a dying downtown. Even G.E. doesn't want to live there any longer. They're pulling out." Sabra lifted her coffee cup, signaling Emmy.

Emmy strode over and poured refills for us both.

"Tell Sabra about Schenectady," I said.

Emmy glanced down the counter. All quiet. She set the pot back on the burner, checked the pins in her careful chignon and asked, "Did I tell you about the park?"

I shook my head no.

And Emmy's voice started, wistful. "There's this park there, Central Park. It's vast and wooded. In the middle there's a pond, and in the middle of the pond, a wooden swan house. You can skate out to it in the winter while the loudspeakers play waltzes. At night, colored lights play over the ice, and skaters drink hot chocolate on a stone patio outside the Casino restaurant. There are two playgrounds, and a fire truck for the children to climb on. Behind the playground, peacocks strut in an aviary. Paul brought me a tail feather one Thanksgiving. It was purply blue with spots on it that really do look like eyes. I lost it," she said with a small toss of her head. "A tiny train runs all day in the summer, round and round a track, and the children don't have to pay money to ride in the passenger cars. It's all free. It chugs through a little tunnel, and the children scream. In the winter, sledding children risk Devil's Cauldron, the hill that drops all the way from the junior high school to the pond "

A bell rang, and Emmy left to pick up her order.

"Well?" I asked.

Sabra unwrapped her hand. "The bird cages smell. The duck house is spattered with shit. The PA system for the loudspeakers crackles, and I don't remember any train."

Before she left, Sabra told me she'd applied for a travel grant. Prospects were good; she might actually get to Tibet.

The next time I sat waiting for Sabra, Emmy told me about the waterfront.

"It's the oldest part of town," she said. "Rich people live there. Stone walls enclose gardens and goldfish ponds. Row houses line bumpy, bricked streets. In a circular courtyard, there's a statue and an old wooden phone booth painted red. The rich people paint their doors bright colors and nail brass numbers to their houses to date them. There's a riverside park where families have picnics. Once, Paul looked in an open door and saw a marble hall with paneled walls and a chandelier. There was a brass letter drop and buzzers in a brass plate, and a porcelain umbrella stand. And that was just the hall. And Paul said ivy climbs over everything, and, in summer, the whole neighborhood smells mossy and green and boats drift by the picnickers." Emmy sighed.

"Did Paul live there?" I asked.

"No, he lived on Division Street in a two-family."

"What did he do?" I asked.

Emmy straightened as she answered, and I understood she'd been proud of her brother, "He was a reporter for the *Gazette*, the *Schenectady Gazette*."

"Any children?"

"No, he never married. He had a girl for a while though, a school-teacher. Nothing came of it. She married someone else." Emmy scowled briefly at the memory of the jilt. "My mother didn't like her." She cut off to take an order.

Waiting, I mused, realizing the descriptions were probably Paul's, possibly to the word. Each year he arrived home, already eager to leave, trying to evoke Schenectady for himself as much as for them. And, during the intervals Paul was away, Emmy preserved the map of Schenectady in her imagination, because Paul lived there, because it was away, because it did not have a concrete floor that made her legs ache. Imagine longing for something so attainable, a wish so easy to grant.

When Sabra arrived, stamping snow from her boots, I told her, "I'm going to buy Emmy a bus ticket."

"What?" Sabra asked, slipping out of her sheepskin coat.

"I'm going to buy Emmy a ticket to Schenectady."

"You can't," Sabra said.

"Why not?"

"Because it isn't what she thinks. I'm telling you—Vonnegut's Mr. Rosewater would not recognize Emmy's Schenectady. I have to tell her what it's really like."

"You can't do that," I said. I set down my spoon. "You really can't do that. She's been dreaming about the place for years."

Sabra shrugged. Only then I noticed her face, not just red from the cold, but shiny, expectant. "Look, the grant came through." She hugged her shoulders. "I'm really going to Tibet."

I congratulated her. I waited, hoping she'd start describing misty mountains, the Dalai Lama, living in spiritual exile here in the U.S. But she didn't.

Instead she said, "It's a great deal. All expenses paid, a generous per diem, and I get to see my heart place to boot."

The following week when I entered the diner, I handed Emmy a bus ticket.

"What's this?"

"A ticket to Schenectady," I said. I kept my eyes on the sugar packet I was tearing open as I asked, "Can you get the time off?"

"Oh, yes," she said.

I raised my eyes then. Emmy was blushing, protesting, "You really shouldn't have. I mean . . ."

Down the counter, Red executed a quarter-turn, taking in the exchange. Embarrassed, I ordered a grilled English to cut the scene short.

Trailing her purple scarf, Sabra banged in. Waiting to order, she thrummed the counter with her mauve-tinted fingernails.

"Nervous?" I asked.

"Busy," she answered.

The conversation was balky. Travel details for the upcoming trip distracted her. Then I confessed.

"I bought Emmy a bus ticket."

Sabra dropped her spoon. "You didn't."

I cast a sidelong peek toward Red who was occupied with his coffee. I nodded.

"Then I've got to warn her what it's really like."

"Don't do that." I grabbed her arm, surprised by my own vehemence. "You can't do that to her. The only time she's ever even been out of the state is to cross the line to New Hampshire. She's never even been to Canada."

"All the more reason," Sabra said, retrieving her spoon. "Think of Gauguin in Tahiti. It's nothing like those happy paradise paintings. He was miserable. He had diarrhea. Sick all the time."

"But if he hadn't gone, he wouldn't have painted those paintings."

Sabra ignored me.

Twice, I tried to interrupt her as she, after summoning Emmy, started painting over Paul's picture of Schenectady with images of ugly Italian restaurants and run-down mill houses and littered playgrounds and smelly park perverts and flashy cretin cars drag racing on Broadway. It wasn't a pretty picture. When I looked at Emmy, her expression composed itself, the always careful lipstick, the eyeliner, drawn just a little more tightly than usual. Then she smiled, thanked Sabra for the information, and tripped off to refill draining coffee cups.

That was the end of my friendship with Sabra. I didn't contact her again before her departure for Tibet. And I didn't regret it, even though I later lost touch with Emmy, too, when I moved out of state. Sabra's series of paintings, "Invocations," begun in Tibet, earned her a favorable review in the *Times*. But I couldn't bring myself to call her, because I hadn't forgiven her for dulling over Emmy and Paul's bright impression of Schenectady.

We stopped meeting for coffee at the diner, but I went back alone to see Emmy. On my first return, she handed me an envelope.

"What's this?" I asked, expecting a thank you note perhaps but not the dollar bills I fanned out in my hand.

"I turned in the ticket," Emmy said, her face coloring beneath her makeup. "That's your refund. It's not that I'm ungrateful. It's one of the nicest things anybody ever did for me. I felt between a rock and, you know, it's just . . ."

I waited as Emmy, without Paul to help her, struggled for the words.

"It's not really my place," she said. "It's Paul's. If I went there, I wouldn't want to go there anymore. It wouldn't be the same."

I nodded. I understood, but I was sad, because I knew in that instant that I'd never be able to go to the Yucatan. I ordered a slice of cherry pie.

Red plopped down next to me and poked his fingers into the bib of his overalls, retrieving his Marlboros. "Gypsy Rose Lee hit the road?" he asked.

"I'm sorry."

"Purple girl," he explained. "She gone?"

I nodded, and he bent a match, flicked it across the flint. "Dig up any trolls yet up there at the hole?"

"What?" I blinked.

"I didn't think so," he said. "Never were any trolls in that damn sinkhole. Just ice. Blocks of ice. I used to be an ice-cutter myself. But it didn't cut no ice with me," he said and laughed at the private joke, then inhaled. "Do you know the problem with ice?"

"No," I said.

Red squinted at me through his smoke. "And you're a college girl. The problem with ice, girl, is: it melts."

He grinned when I laughed.

When Emmy returned with the slice, an oversized slice, she winked. "You know that coffee emporium I told you about? Did I tell you that it had wide board floors and curved glass cases?" she asked. "The owner also sold willowware ginger jars full of crystallized ginger."

Apparently, Sabra's revision hadn't altered Emmy's vision.

I forked my pie, as Emmy unwrapped the small treasures of Schenectady, New York, wondering how I was going to persuade her to accompany me to Montreal. We could go up on the train. It was a pretty trip along Lake Champlain. We could see a play, a movie, eat at one of the French restaurants. I'm sorry that we never got to go. I received the research position in New York state shortly thereafter, at the university, not too far from Schenectady. I've been here a few years, but I've never driven over. I might someday when I can spare the time. If I do, I'll send Emmy a Victorian postcard if the store on Jay Street is still there.

DEVIL'S FIDDLE

BEFORE AGGIE'S GRAY HAIR earned her the anonymous respectability of age, she was the town pump. And before the Howell boys' surprising survival to their twenties when they found jobs and wives and became active in the Volunteer Fire Department and the Odd Fellows and the Beaumont Historical Society, they were terrors. A singularity marked both Aggie and the Howell boys that townspeople respected. Most Beaumonters cut wide and glad paths around craziness and meanness. Any fool but a Howell could have guessed that those two singular forces were meant to sidestep each other. But the Howell boys went out of their way to bump into Aggie's madness.

No one knew much about Aggie. She had outlived her history and most townspeople's memory of it in the parsonage house in the center of the village. No one could remember exactly how she had come to reside in the parsonage house. Minister Gray, like his father, the first Minister Gray, lived in the frame house across from the lake. Aggie lived in the parsonage and, from all appearances, she intended to stay, her tenancy deeded to her by the accumulated weight of personal belongings that had overflowed onto the porch and yard: a vintage late-forties washer/wringer, a Frigidaire, two sagging couches, sundry doors and pane-less windows, a rusty freezer, stovepipe, guttering, copper pipe and rolls of chicken netting and snow fence. Aggie clearly intended to stay.

Seldom visible in town, she had Wayne Wright deliver her groceries from the Beaumont General Store. The only car she owned had been getting unbeatable mileage for decades—a blue Falcon perched on blocks in the front yard. Occasionally, townspeople could glimpse Aggie

119

White through a window, her face pinched and pale and framed with the spikes of her sparse white hair like a ghastly angel in a rummage sale halo. A glimpse could lurk in the imagination for weeks. To step on Aggie's scraggly lawn qualified as the test of bravery for village kids. As neglected as the lawn appeared, a footfall, even a toe-fall, could summon Aggie, nightdress flapping, screeching onto her porch, kicking aside machine parts as she raced to her lawn's defense. Aggie White was the acknowledged town eccentric, but in a town populated by them, no one wanted to initiate the round of finger-pointing, so people pretty much left Aggie alone.

Everyone knew about the Howell boys. Their histories, remarkably rich for ones so young, distinguished them. Howells popped up everywhere they shouldn't—in Roy Davis's bull pen, in the magazine shelf behind the counter where Wayne Wright stashed the *Hustlers* and *Playboys*, in the schoolhouse during Christmas vacation, in the beer tent at the county fair.

Among the alleged crimes attributed to the Howell boys were: the hog-tying of all the baby goats at the Osgood farm, the half-sawn legs of Fat Annie the blind fiddler's chair at the street dance, the mysterious appearance of the centerfolds glued to all the Methodists' windshields during Easter service, and the coincidental disappearance on the previous Good Friday of Wayne Wright's entire stock of men's magazines, the barn-burning at Spindle farm, and the quarter-wit child born to the Garlinghouses' half-wit daughter. But the Garlinghouses did not confront the Howells. Nor did the fire marshall. Nor Wayne Wright. Nor the sheriff. No one confronted the Howells.

The Howells lived at the edge of town and the law. Their porch matched Aggie's for innovative exterior decorating—gun racks and deer racks, all of your major and minor appliances, pulleys, come-alongs, tire chains, and the inventory for several used auto parts stores. No one stepped into Howells' grass-bare yard without an invitation, second thoughts, and well-concealed misgivings. The Howells were the best hunters in town. They were also argumentative. A Winchester barrel is a very persuasive point of view. The best hunters in Beaumont, the Howells lived fervently by their credo that to everything there is a season. And that season lasted all year. Howells, jackers and poachers by genetic inheritance, were not particular about their game. Visitors exiting the Howells' generally walked backwards to their cars. When locals discussed the Howells' latest misadventure, they mumbled about the high-spiritedness of youth, how boys will be boys and Howells will be Howells. So when the three Howell boys began tormenting Aggie, no one intervened with what was generally perceived as a fulfillment of their biological destinies: to be as mean and as stupid as bull moose in rutting season. But even the Howells proved to be educable.

The torment of Aggie began with a lackluster occasional stone through the window, pissing brown spots into the beloved lawn, strapping a dead buck to the hood of the blue Falcon, and arc-welding the horseshoes of Rugged, Roy Davis's Morgan horse, to the Frigidaire on the front porch with the horse still attached. (Rest in peace, Rugged.) Mischief, by Howell standards, about as annoying as a logy housefly. And the three boys, Buck, Buckly, and Chuck (the Howells compensated for their superabundant instinct for practical jokery with a completely deficient imagination for anything verging on the literate, including naming) usually celebrated their latest prank sipping underage Buds stolen from Wayne Wright's cooler and joking with the sheriff. Short of murder, Buck, Buckly, and Chuck could get away with anything.

As the game warden, I had a particular interest in the Howells. After the state restocked the lake with trout, the Howell boys reputedly dynamited it and netted the entire restocking effort. The Howells ate steak the year Roy Davis experimented with a switch from dairy cows to beef cattle. When swish New York restaurants discovered grilled venison, the Howells' unregistered trucks ran night and day for a year. Their freezers were bottomless. When the fickle New York diet switched to pheasant out of the game bird season, Howells had the most surprising luck with treadless roadkill.

I respected the Howells in the way I respected the first animal I ever shot—a fat raccoon who'd mistaken my mother's garden for a diner. That raccoon had torn down three fences with its claws. And it had eaten so much corn, it bulged as round as a small bear. I feared that animal. I respected that animal. I admired that animal's ingenuity even as I cornered it in the grain barn. The damn creature rocked back onto its hind legs ready to have at me, and I shot it. I was exhilarated, and sickened, and elated, and saddened by its death. That covers how I felt about the Howells. As the game warden, I stalked them, but not too closely because I wasn't sure what I would do with them if I did catch them. But I did want to catch them, and that was how I came to witness their harassment of Aggie who usually obliged them by blinking out the window with her doe eyes and frazzled hair, a perfect target, as another stone struck the glass. By flicking on the interior lights, she helped the Howells with their aim. When she caught them urinating on the lawn, Aggie delighted them with a full-blown screech and flapping nightdress appearance on the front porch, her gray hair tugged out like horns from her head. Annually, Beaumont children who had heard Aggie's screech tossed sleepless in their beds on October thirty-first. But not the Howell boys, who just enjoyed a few more sticky-fingered Buds and a slumber a six-pack more stuporous than usual.

That particular Halloween Buck, Buckly, and Chuck, then about fourteen, fifteen, and sixteen, had everybody on edge. Wayne Wright's cooler at the general store towered with egg cartons, not a single dozen missing. The overstocked cans of Barbasol gathered dust on the shelves in cosmetics. Wayne grew so fidgety waiting for the boys to steal something that he finally tossed them a carton of Camels, soaped his own windows, splattered a few eggs on his pickup, locked up, and went to bed. So as not to disappoint anyone, Buck, Buckly, and Chuck stove in a few jack-o'-lanterns with their steel-toed boots and stole a couple of trick-or-treat bags from the grade school kids. Cruel but not inspired. Beaumont expects more from its legends.

I was sitting in my car in front of the store, smoking and waiting. After a while I looked sidelong out the window. Buck, Buckly, and Chuck, in black jeans and black T-shirts, their faces sooted with candleblack, stared back at me. In their smudgepot faces, their eyes waxed unnaturally white and round. "You kids have any plans for Halloween?" I asked.

"Yeah. Yeah," Buck said. "We thought we might go up to the party at the school and bob for cheerleaders. Yum. Yum. Love those pompoms." Buck smacked his lips.

"Heh. Heh," Buckly and Chuck sniggered. "Yeah. Love those pom-poms."

Cute kids. Wit, the pride of Beaumont. I stubbed my cigarette in the ashtray and lit another. The Howell boys huddled and whispered, flashed open their hunting jackets, patted their pockets. Something was going down. When they sauntered off, I followed them after a safe interval. I suspected concealed weapons, some planned target practice up at Davis's saltlick. The innocence of their intended mischief took me by surprise.

It was a perfect fall night. Hunter's moon. As many stars in the sky as leaves on the ground. A heavy dew hushed the leaves underfoot as I followed the boys past the lake. The cool, clear perfection of the air, sharp and pepperminty, snapped me awake, so alert my nerves tingled ten years off my life. I almost didn't mind being out at night, tailing the Howell boys.

Ahead of me the boys sharp-scissored their silhouettes against the moon. Their blade-thin shadows cut to a stop at the crest of the hill in front of Minister Gray's. I ducked behind a blue spruce in the churchyard. A ground-creeping yellow fog welled in the hollows. I squinted. Buck or Buckly slithered on his stomach between Mrs. Gray's tidy flower beds, across the croquet court, under the garden settee up to Minister Gray's house, holding something carefully in his hand as he pulled himself forward on cocked elbows. When he reached the house, he fiddled around the foundation clapboards, crouched, then slunk back to the other two. The other Buck or Buckly dug something out of his pocket, handed it to Chuck, who began waving it back and forth, over and over in the air like he was blessing the grass. They all hunkered down in the skeletal lilac bushes, laughing a whispery laugh. I couldn't figure out what they were up to until I heard the sound I hadn't heard since my own childhood.

At first the sound echoed soft and natural, a forest sound, like a branch groaning. Then the noise rasped, grated, wood grinding wood. Insisting on its unnaturalness, louder and louder, it hummed and whined. Lights blinked on in Minister Gray's house. Aside from that unearthly noise, the night brooded so quiet that I could hear Mrs. Gray's thin voice say, "Go see who it is, Gary. Find out what they want." A few more lights. That unearthly thrumming and then a descent down the staircase that was slower than any reluctant penitent's to hell. The front door flew open, and Minister Gray in his bathrobe thrust out a weak flashlight and a crucifix and hollered, "Get thee behind me."

I suppressed a laugh. For a Methodist minister, it was one hell of a flashy show of faith. Squatting behind that spruce, I felt a communion with the acrid fir smell, the scrub-clean scent of the stars, the still-sweet compost of the leaves and even with the spirit of the Howell boys, quietly choking on their laughter in the blind of the lilac bushes.

Satisfied he'd stared down Satan or scared witless himself, Minister Gray slammed the door. The lights blinked off. After a pause, Buck or Buckly slithered forward again, wrapping the slacked fishing line around his fist as he inched along to retrieve the shingling nail from the clapboard. The other Buck/Buckly tucked the resin back into the breast pocket of his hunting jacket. The three huddled and snickered. Watching them, I remembered how sixteen felt at night, like nature had invented the world and its secrets for you alone, how it felt to feel your calf muscles flex, your nostrils siphon the air into your lungs, to hear the huff of your own breath, to feel like the greatest secret in a world of secrets—a shadow in a shapeless coat stalking your solitude in the darkness. Damn. I didn't trust those boys one bit more, but I almost liked them.

That was before I realized where they were headed next. I followed them up Lake Road to the fork where they legged left across the Chadwicks' lawn and crouched in the shadow of the blue Falcon. They planned to devil's-fiddle Aggie. Devil's-fiddling a single, senile recluse on Halloween didn't strike me as good sport. But I underestimated Aggie.

Buck/Buckly slid around the discarded washers and ice boxes, and rolls of chicken wire, up to the house and shoved the nail under a bottom clapboard. The other Buck/Buckly and Chuck yanked the line taut and started running the resin back and forth. The parsonage started to vibrate and moan before it threw its whole wooden studded soul and frame into a hair-bristling wail. By the moonlight, I watched the cows in Roy Davis's pasture roll onto their backs and poke their legs into the sky like they were playing dead. The fiddle keened. The Howell boys chuckled as a light winked on in the house. One, two upstairs windows checkerboarded the darkness with light. The palladian window on the stairwell arched with light. Snap, snap. The two front parlor windows filled with light. I could see Aggie's backlit profile as she peered out, probably scared out of her senses. I was about to disclose myself, say, "Okay, boys, enough fun for the night," when the lights downstairs flicked off. One two. The palladian window blacked out. Only the two upstairs windows remained lit.

"What the hey—?" Buck said.

"Yeah," Buckly agreed.

Chuck fiddled full-tilt then, working back and forth over the fishing line.

"Way to go, Ground Chuck. Make mincemeat out of that baby," Buck encouraged him in a low voice.

"Yeah. Way to go, Woodchuck," Buckly coached. "Let's scare the old girl right out of her panties." By night's end, Buckly would conclude that he had a near-miss gift for prophecy.

The fiddle howled like a banshee, crunched like dead leaves underfoot, hooted like an owl, rasped like a saw. The resin, warmed by the friction, grew gummy, ran hot over Chuck's hand, sizzled his skin. "Damn," he cursed and wiped his hand on the seat of his jeans, but he kept grimly at it.

Huddled in the dark, listening to that eerie chorus, I wondered about its power. What could that music summon? I can only speculate about Buck, Buckly, and Chuck's expectations: that Aggie would call the sheriff, or come flapping out in her nightdress, that the old parsonage would shiver itself into a pile of sawdust, that the dead would peel from their graves in the churchyard. I can only guess, but I am positive that none of us expected what happened next.

As Buck sweated over the wire, a thin voice wailed out over the fiddle, "Gary, that you?" A momentary pause, then, "Gary, you're the same as your father. The sixteen-year-olds always come back. Nobody forgets his first time." Then another, longer pause.

"Gary?" Buck asked. Chuck bent his back to the fiddle. The porch light glared. The door of the parsonage banged open, and Aggie White teetered onto the front porch in red high heels.

Whatever we expected, none of us expected Aggie to dance. But Aggie danced. Beaumont may have forgotten that, in her prime, Aggie, had been the town pump, but Aggie had not.

With her red sequined teddy sagging over her breasts, and her garters slack over the cheese flesh of her thighs, and her moth-eaten plumage drooping in sympathy over her drooping buttocks, Aggie began to shimmy. She shimmied until, skinny as she was, her loose flesh shimmied like a second self around her, a snake's skin she could slither right out of. She shimmied, lifting her arms forward and up, shouting, "Come on. Don't be shy. Let's dance."

Long after Buck, agape, had dropped the rosin and slacked the line, Aggie hopped and spun and thrust to soundless music. The sparse tufts of her white hair pricked and pointed and bobbed and dipped. Her chicken legs kicked and crossed. Her buttocks swung and swayed. Her hips swiveled. Her arms flailed. She shivered and shook and shimmied until her sequins sproinged off and she danced in a glinting blizzard. And then it happened.

Dancing to the devil's fiddle, Aggie's flesh began to renounce gravity. Her thighs plumped up. Her calves muscled. Her buttocks girdled themselves into place until the ostrich feathers snapped to attention. Her breasts swelled. The garters tightened. The bodice overflowed. The white hair reflected the light of the sequins, thickened, lengthened, tumbled over her shoulders. A beautifully young Aggie pumped her pelvis so slowly it was as untrackable as the movement of the earth, the moon, the stars. Then the old young girl bent over and adjusted the seams of her stockings, straightened up and began to sing. It took me a moment to recognize the melody, but, when I did, the hairs on my forearms bristled. Note for note, Aggie was singing back to us the random score of the Howells' devil's fiddle. Perfect pitch, clear to the stars.

The music summoned her partner, skinny as a shadow, black and flittery as a bat. He seemed more a paper cutout than a person, his hair tufting up at the temples like the horns of a crescent moon. He clasped Aggie in his shadow arms, and they waltzed over the porch floor to the click, click of only one pair of heels as if Aggie's partner's feet were slippered. When I glanced at the man's feet, I could swear by Rugged's memory, they were hooves. But moonlight is a clever magician.

At the appearance of Aggie's suitor, the slack-jawed Howell boys tested their rubbery lips.

"Mother of God," Buck said.

"In a pig's eye," Buckly said.

"I'm history," Chuck said. And the three of them burned skidmarks into Aggie's lawn, speeding out of there. Under the circumstances, it struck me as wise to follow their lead.

All Saints' Day dawned on Aggie, scrawny and fretful, yanking at her white hair and transplanting crabgrass into the bare marks in her lawn before retreating behind her barricade of obsolete appliances. Same as ever.

But the Howell boys changed. Wayne Wright at the General Store said, "Someone overheard the Howell boys going on about somebody up to Aggie's. Who the devil was up there last night?"

"Yes," I said.

Wayne scratched his head. But in a town of eccentrics, we develop an instinct for backing off.

Buck married the half-wit girl who'd borne his child, and together they populated Beaumont with a brood of fractions. Buckly became respectable, one of the best artificial inseminators in the state, which permitted Roy Davis to permanently pasture his bull and the locals to get in a few digs about the girls Buckly had bred over the years before his transformation. Chuck became the Landfill Supervisor (a.k.a. the dump man) and founder and chairman of the Beaumont Historical Society. I resigned as game warden. Without the Howell boys to stalk, the job no longer felt sporting. The timing felt right to break from the past. I'm thinking of starting a vintage car restoration business. Maybe Aggie would consider selling me that blue Falcon.

The Howell boys lead clean lives now. But if I were those boys, I'd keep one eye cocked over my shoulder. Sometimes our connection to the past stretches as thin as a fishing line, but it has a way of reeling you in. The past can dance up on you. You can never completely spurn it. Just look at our porches.

WHEN MOUNTAINS MOVE

WHEN MY FATHER ENTERS the kitchen, my mother smoothly shifts to another topic. I have just finished asking her if her scalp itches. Her hair is growing back—a gray as soft as mown hay, weathering in an October field. Silver thatch.

"Oh no," she says. "Never let a dog bully you. They sniff fear. If Carey acts afraid, just tell him to keep walking right on by." Only her finger twisting a shock of her short hair betrays her insincerity. "That's the only way Carey will overcome his fear of that dog."

Carey is my two-year-old son. The dog is imaginary.

My mother's elbows press against the nicked surface of the kitchen table. Affecting casualness, she rests her chin on her hands, her head swaying slightly in the hammock of her interlaced fingers. "Hi dear," she greets my father breezily and smiles. But, suspicious and baffled, he stares at her. He stands in the door frame, his hair uncombed, his shirt tail untucked, his elbows cocked—sharp as accusations. "What are you two talking about?" he asks too abruptly.

"Conquering the fear of dogs," my mother says. She sips at her now cold cup of coffee. Its surface shimmers with an iridescent skim, floating like a gas stain on a rain-slicked parking lot. She swallows.

"The hell you were," my father snaps. The tail of his shirt flaps as he pivots and bolts from the room.

My mother sighs. I smile in sympathy. It is all I find to offer her now. When Mom called to share her latest doctor's report with me, I packed up my sympathy, my bags, Carey. "I'm going to stay with my mother," I told Curt. "Perhaps your parents would rather be alone right now," he said. But I knew my father. My mother would need me. Three weeks ago, my mother decided, "No more chemo."

My father raged for a week. "Suicide," he said. "It's suicide plain and simple. How can you do this to me? To you?"

"Do what," my mother answered. "I'm not doing anything. I've just decided not to do. No more chemo."

Her resolve confounds him. My father stamps around the house, bewildered by her courage or cowardice; he is not certain which. I want to extend sympathy. But when he brushes back his bafflement like the gray hair from his eyes, he stares at my mother and me, his eyes scouting the trail of our conversation for the unmistakable sign of our conspiratorial morbidity—the bent twig, the clear print that will lead him to us in our guilt—treed.

My mother pushes herself up from the table and pours her coffee down the sink drain. She reaches for a dishcloth and dabs at a spill on the white porcelain. She keeps rubbing the spot long after it is dry while she stares out the window at the jagged ring of perse mountains.

Her voice startles me. "You know, your father's acting as if I'm leaving him for another man," she says, then laughs a short, embarrassed laugh. "I think he's jealous."

"He feels excluded," I say.

My mother stands very still. "Excluded? Well, it's good practice," she says. In the tangy, autumn air, the words sting. I try to warm my hands on the porcelain mug, now cold. My mother continues, "He thinks it's all you and I ever talk about, death and dying. He thinks it's all I think about."

My father would be surprised. We talk mainly about life, about Carey, or some memory that we've refined over the years into a one-liner sure to provoke an easy laugh. Remember that time when we lived in that tract development and Dad entered the wrong house, yelled, "Honey, Sugar Bear's home." Remember the time we took the train all the way to New York to pick up the car and you forgot the keys . . . remember. But these memories have an urgency now that belies the easy laugh.

My mother interrupts my memories with a sentence almost clairvoyant. "Of course," she says, still staring out the window, "your father isn't all wrong. My life is about death now." And then she snaps the dish rag briskly as if irritated by her own melodrama. "Let's sit outside. It's warmer outside this time of year, and there's precious little sun in the mountains anyway."

Carey is up from his nap. My mother and I sit in recliners on the front lawn, watching him scuffle through the leaves tangled in the high grass. Dad's let the lawn go. No point mowing this time of year, he says, first frost will be any night now. He's right; its nearness tingles in the air. The trees sense it. Squirrels bury acorns in the meadow. But the mountains shunt the omens aside, shoulder up, purple, against the sky. They can bear what winter hurls at them. Permanent, proud, they shun time. Through all seasons, green, purple, white, they bear up.

I glance at my mother. Her eyes, clear and dark, reflect the sky. Clouds scud across them. The cold of the ground hunkers beneath the webbed recliner. But the late afternoon sun warms my chest, my arms. For a second, I am almost glad to be here in the only place that has ever signified home; then I remember why I am here. I shiver as I watch Carey spike some leaves on a stick.

"I love it here this time of year," I say aside to my mother. "It's so beautiful . . . something to do with the slant of light."

My mother flashes me a look of impatience. I wonder if I should change the subject, but, stupidly, I press on. "The way the light falls, so purple—light, air, and color seem all one element."

My mother closes her eyes. Her mouth puckers in kiss-lines. But I can't stop talking; survival suddenly depends on talking. "I wish Carey could grow up here," I say. "It's such a great place to raise kids. Outdoors where they can run. No one to bother."

My mother jerks up, snaps the back of her recliner straight. "Stop talking nonsense," she says. "We all wish. Wish. Wish. Wishes. Why is everyone so wishy?"

I shade my eyes, hiding them from her. I don't know the answer.

"Wishy," she repeats. "Wishy, wishy, wishy-washy."

I improvise, "If wishes were horses, beggars could ride." Nonsense language. She speaks it.

My mother laughs a long, natural laugh, and I join her. Carey looks up and laughs, too. He toddles toward us, his hands full of plucked grass, and throws it at my mother's legs. She flicks the blades aside with a cursory brush of her fingertips and asks, "Why doesn't anyone know how to talk to me anymore? Why especially now?"

My eyes sting. "No one knows what to say, Mom. No one knows the right response."

"Right response," she parrots. "There is no right response to death. You make it up as you go along."

Again I have no answer for her. Uneasy and quiet, I huddle into my chair. Her eyes darken so blue, so purple that she could hide in their shade. They shine with privacy, a turning inward like the secrecy that glints in pregnant women's eyes—as if all meaning were interior.

"At least your father gets angry," my mother complains, but her voice is mild. "At least your father reacts, confronts the hard truth of all this." She picks a blade of grass from her pants leg, begins chewing it. "You always were evasive, even as a child."

I want to shout at her. "This isn't evasion. This is empathy. Talk my ear off. Cut me with resentments hidden and honed for thirty or forty years. Just tell me everything; let me feel it, too." But I do not. She's got enough on her mind. Instead, I watch Carey trundle into a pile of leaves banked against the snow fence. This spring, Dad didn't bother to roll it up.

My mother's right hand curves like a visor over her eyes as she studies Carey. "He doesn't remind me much of you," she says.

I nod. "Still, it's odd," I say, my tone self-consciously neutral, conversational. "When Carey was born, the instant I saw his face, I recognized him. I knew his face like I know my own. It sounds impossible, but I felt as if he were someone I'd grown up, known forever."

My mother's hand drops from her eyes. Her neck cords tense. Alert, her eyes fix on me. "What?" she asks. "What did you say?" Her eyes so bright they scorch me. "I only said that when Carey was born I felt as if . . ."

She nods her head vigorously, cutting me off. "Yes," she says, "that is what it's like. Since I decided to stop the chemo, every instant feels like that, prescient somehow, familiar. Dying feels like that, the unknown known." As she says this, she folds her hands in her lap, a gesture of completeness.

I close my eyes in relief and panic—relief that, at last, I know we can talk about it directly, and panic that I will not find the courage, that our time, what could be our last time together, will slip away from me.

"I feel," my mother's voice slices through my panic, "I feel like an embarrassment."

My back stiffens. I listen to my mother's voice as I open my eyes. Carey flails about in the leaves. His small sky rains yellow maple. When they land, he scoops them up and tosses them over and over again.

"I feel as if I've done something dreadfully embarrassing, indelicate, in choosing not to have any more chemo." My mother's voice rises and falls in prayerful rhythm. "Your father thinks I have chosen to die, but I have not. I have only chosen—no more chemo. It makes me so tired, unnaturally tired, not like illness or fatigue." She sucks her lower lip, then continues, "I cannot choose, none of us can choose, not to die. We die. But I can choose not to drag myself around, bone-tired and too spent to care. I can choose to remember my last days . . . not that I'll be able to remember . . . I mean; I don't know." She falters in momentary confusion, then says, "It's my decision. And I think that decision embarrasses your father and you."

"No, Mom," I protest. But she hushes me by raising her palm.

"But that isn't what matters," she says. "What matters is that I embarrass myself, like I've let myself down, lugging this old body around, this body that has failed me. My mind. My will. This split in me . . . I just . . . deep embarrassment, not fear. That's all. I just wanted you to know. I really can't explain. It's just embarrassment of body, nothing more."

I cannot look at my mother. I do not think I can say anything to her. But I hear my voice, a little choked and strangled, but still my voice, telling her, "Mom, Christmas Eve, last Christmas Eve, Curtis left the gate unlatched. I didn't know it was unlatched. I was carrying boxes out to the van. I thought Carey was inside playing with some measuring cups in the kitchen. Then I saw his back, just a glimpse, disappear through the gate. Time shrank. I dropped the packages and screamed. Then my legs found themselves running, stretching out. I reached the sidewalk. All this happening in a heartbeat. No time to think, only to watch Carey's legs fly off the curb into the cars. Hundreds of cars. I looked, saw the cars bearing down on Carey. And I screamed and waved my arms. A yellow Checker cab, a bus, a red Mustang, I remember the red Mustang, a motorcycle . . . I could have rushed in. I could have dodged into the traffic after Carey. I should have. But I did not. I could not. Something prevented me. I ran back and forth along the sidewalk, my arms flapping, my voice clucking, 'Oh my God. Oh my God.' But I did not try to cross the lanes of traffic. I heard horns, the screech of brakes. My thighs bumped against the fenders. My arms wrapped around Carey. I cried, knowing that I would never look in a mirror again without wondering who I was. I can pretend I was paralyzed by fear, but I distinctly remember pacing back and forth along the road. I chose myself over my son." My voice winds down. My hands wipe at my wet, salty face. When I raise my head, my mother's eyes attack mine with a clear ferocity.

"Then you know," she says. Her hand reaches and finds mine. "It's the exact opposite. But it's really the same. In letting my body go, I choose myself over you. It's really what we all have to do—choose ourselves. But we cannot help but feel the dreadful inadequacy of our choice." She shakes her head.

I think of my father's rumpled shirt, his uncombed hair. "Dad feels it too," I whisper.

"I know. I know that," my mother says. Her sweater rises, falls. She cries soundlessly.

We fall quiet, watching the light tilt from the sky, the purple shadows glide in like kites catching a downdraft from the mountains. Tatters of maple leaves stick to Carey's sweater. A raggedy patchwork scarecrow, he twists and twirls in the wind, striking the heads off the dark aster with his stick. The wind riles up the leaves. They spin like children, dizzying themselves until they drop. Even the stones grow souls this time of year.

"Wouldn't it be wonderful to be like that?" Mom asks me nodding at Carey. "He's like a puppy at play. No self-consciousness."

"Or all self-consciousness," I say.

My mother glances at me, a fleeting but penetrating look, familiar to me since before I can remember, when I first looked at her face and she looked back at me this meaning: I know you. I have always known you.

God forgive me, but how will I ever know myself without her eyes' regard?

Memories open themselves to me. I remember my father giving me a geography lesson at the kitchen table, stabbing the map with a pencil: we live here, he said, in this section of the Appalachian range. Our meadow was probably once ocean floor, accumulating layers of sediment until two continents collided and the momentum folded up the land as if it were a dinner napkin. Imagine that. But I did not believe him. I did not believe that anything so stable, so immutable could fold. But now I know it's true. I know that rocks grow restless, that mountains move.

The screen door slaps. My father, shirt tail flapping, stands on the porch looking down on us. He sniffs the air suspiciously, or perhaps he is only breathing in the sad, perfect smell of apples rotting and, from somewhere far away, the smoke of red leaves burning. He spots Carey in the leaf pile and lopes over to him. Wordlessly he buries him in armful after armful of golden leaves. Carey laughs.

Acknowledgments

"CAMP" FIRST APPEARED in *Treasure House*. "The Attic," "When Mountains Move," "The Ten Joyful Mysteries of the One True Faith," and "A Hard Place" first appeared in *Blueline*. "Good Neighbors" first appeared in *The Worcester Review*. "Aaron's Rod" first appeared in *The Dominion Review*.

The author wishes to thank the following for their assistance with editing stories in the collection: Lisa Ruffolo, Tony Ardizzone, and Gladys Swan. She also wishes to thank Yaddo for giving her the time to work on stories in the collection.

ABOUT THE AUTHOR

Jeff Friedman

Joan Connor is Assistant Professor of
Creative Writing at Ohio University in
Athens.